Dance Class

SPLASHH

Crip • Art

Béka • Story

Maëla Cosson • Color

PAPERCUTZ™

New York

Dance Class Graphic Novels Available from PAPERCUTZ

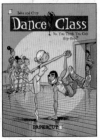

#1 "So, You Think You Can Hip-Hop?"

#2 "Romeos and Juliet"

#3 "African Folk Dance Fever"

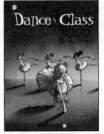

#4 "A Funny Thing Happened on the Way to Paris..."

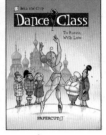

#5 "To Russia, With Love"

#6 "A Merry Olde Christmas"

#7 "School Night Fever"

#8 "Snow White and the Seven Dwarves"

#9 "Dancing in the Rain"

Studio Danse [Dance Class], by Béka & Crip
© 2015 BAMBOO ÉDITION.
www.bamboo.fr
All other editorial material © 2016 by Papercutz.

DANCE CLASS #9
"Dancing in the Rain"

Béka · Writer
Crip · Artist
Maëla Cosson · Colorist
Joe Johnson · Translation
Tom Orzechowski · Lettering
Dawn K. Guzzo— Production
Rachel Pinnelas— Production Coordiantor
Jeff Whitman— Editor
Jim Salicrup
Editor-in-Chief

ISBN: 978-1-62991-187-8

Printed in China
November 2016 by CP printing Ltd.

Papercutz books may be purchased for business or promotional use. For information on bulk purchases please contact Macmillan Corporate and Premium Sales Department at (800) 221-7945 x5442.

Distributed by Macmillan
First Papercutz Printing

DANCE CLASS graphic novels are available for $10.99 each only in hardcover. Available from booksellers everywhere. You can also order online from papercutz.com or call 1-800-886-1223, Monday through Friday, 9 - 5 EST. MC, Visa, and AmEx accepted. To order by mail, please add $4.00 for postage and handling for first book ordered, $1.00 for each additional book and make check payable to NBM Publishing. Send to: Papercutz, 160 Broadway, Suite 700, East Wing, New York, NY 10038.

DANCE CLASS graphic novels are also available digitally wherever e-books are sold.

Papercutz.com

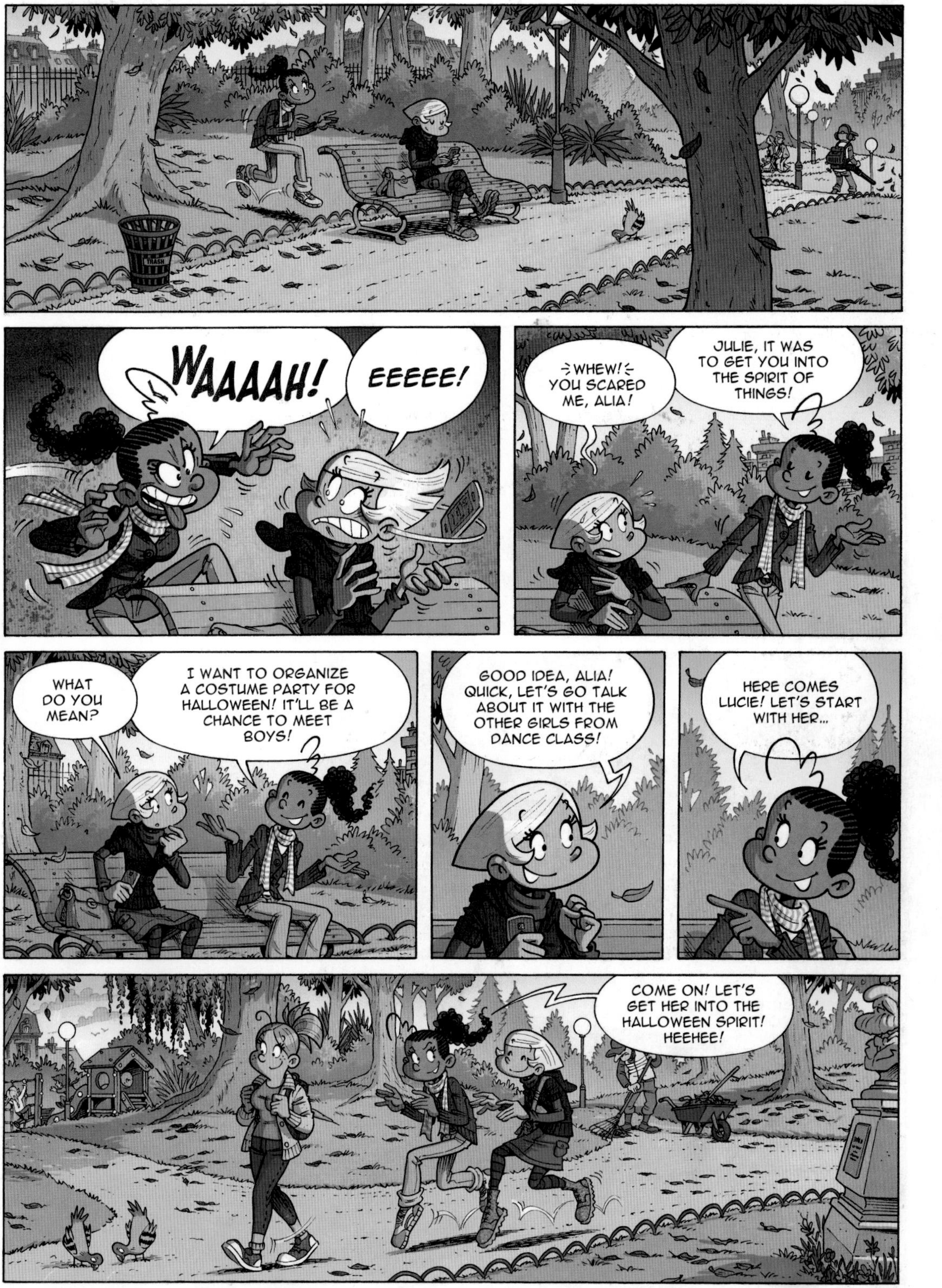
WAAAAH!
EEEEE!
WHEW! YOU SCARED ME, ALIA!
JULIE, IT WAS TO GET YOU INTO THE SPIRIT OF THINGS!
WHAT DO YOU MEAN?
I WANT TO ORGANIZE A COSTUME PARTY FOR HALLOWEEN! IT'LL BE A CHANCE TO MEET BOYS!
GOOD IDEA, ALIA! QUICK, LET'S GO TALK ABOUT IT WITH THE OTHER GIRLS FROM DANCE CLASS!
HERE COMES LUCIE! LET'S START WITH HER...
COME ON! LET'S GET HER INTO THE HALLOWEEN SPIRIT! HEEHEE!

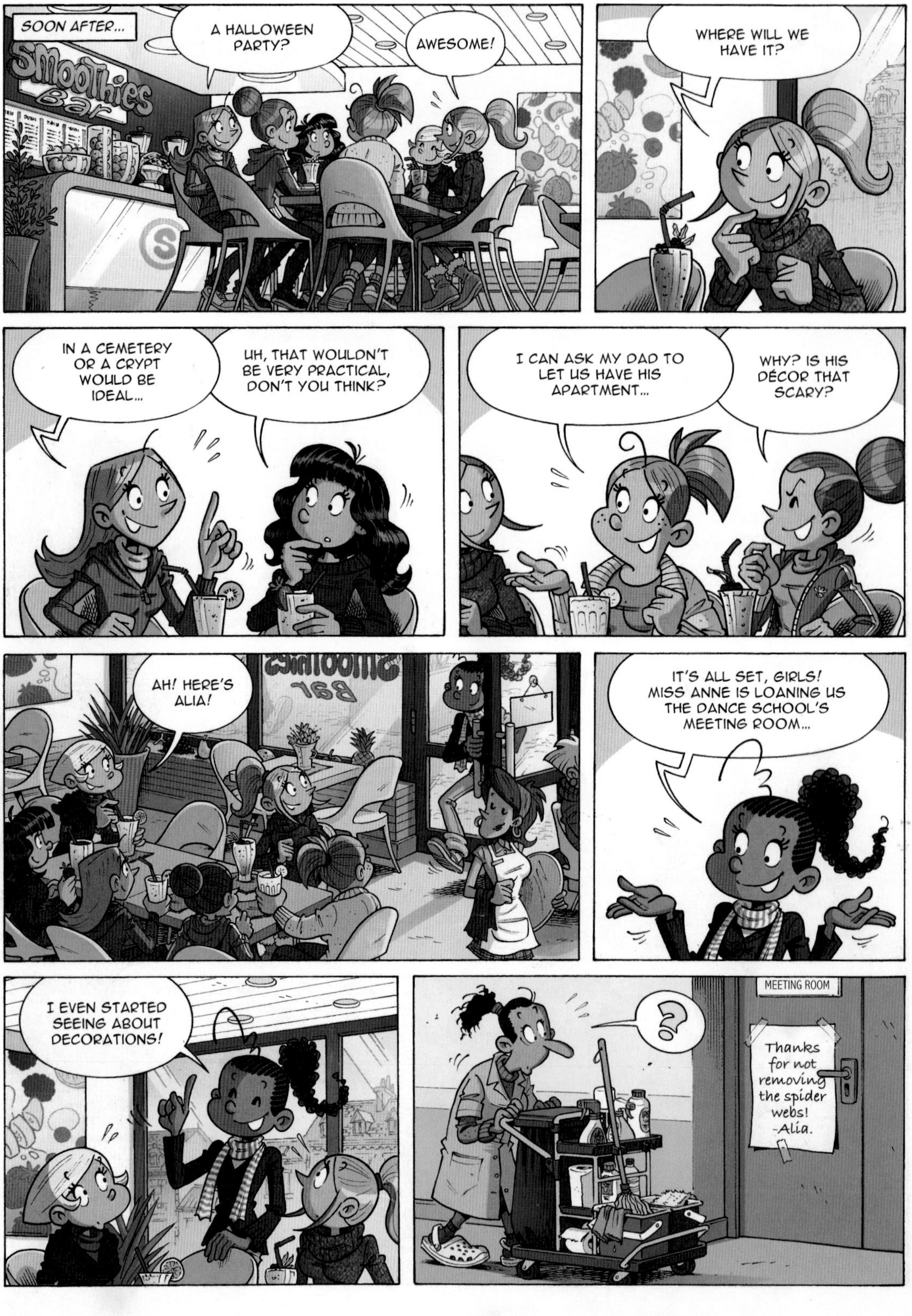

SOON AFTER...
A HALLOWEEN PARTY?
AWESOME!
WHERE WILL WE HAVE IT?
IN A CEMETERY OR A CRYPT WOULD BE IDEAL...
UH, THAT WOULDN'T BE VERY PRACTICAL, DON'T YOU THINK?
I CAN ASK MY DAD TO LET US HAVE HIS APARTMENT...
WHY? IS HIS DÉCOR THAT SCARY?
AH! HERE'S ALIA!
IT'S ALL SET, GIRLS! MISS ANNE IS LOANING US THE DANCE SCHOOL'S MEETING ROOM...
I EVEN STARTED SEEING ABOUT DECORATIONS!
?
MEETING ROOM
Thanks for not removing the spider webs! -Alia.

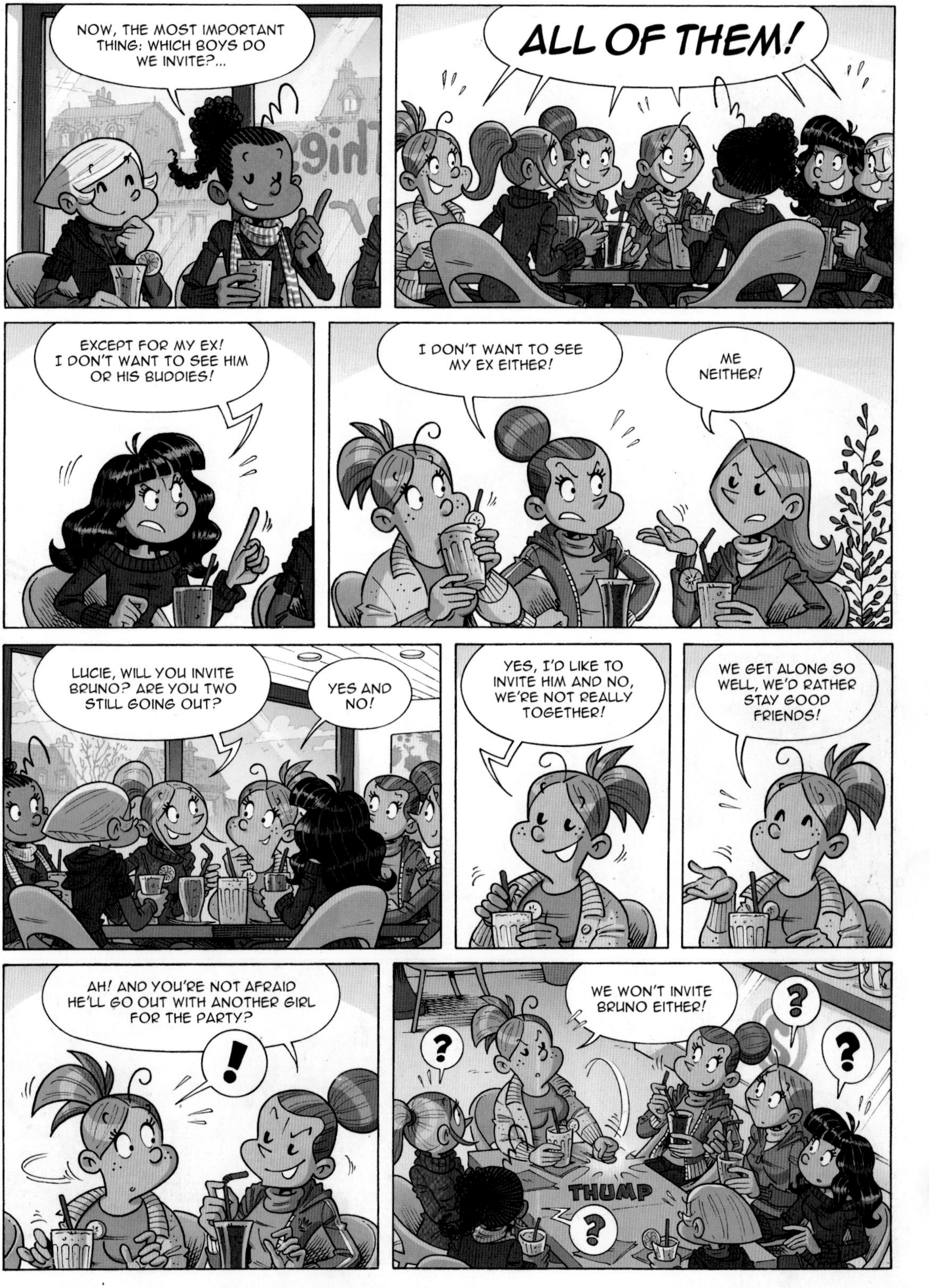
NOW, THE MOST IMPORTANT THING: WHICH BOYS DO WE INVITE?...
ALL OF THEM!
EXCEPT FOR MY EX! I DON'T WANT TO SEE HIM OR HIS BUDDIES!
I DON'T WANT TO SEE MY EX EITHER!
ME NEITHER!
LUCIE, WILL YOU INVITE BRUNO? ARE YOU TWO STILL GOING OUT?
YES AND NO!
YES, I'D LIKE TO INVITE HIM AND NO, WE'RE NOT REALLY TOGETHER!
WE GET ALONG SO WELL, WE'D RATHER STAY GOOD FRIENDS!
AH! AND YOU'RE NOT AFRAID HE'LL GO OUT WITH ANOTHER GIRL FOR THE PARTY?
!
WE WON'T INVITE BRUNO EITHER!
?
?
?
THUMP
?

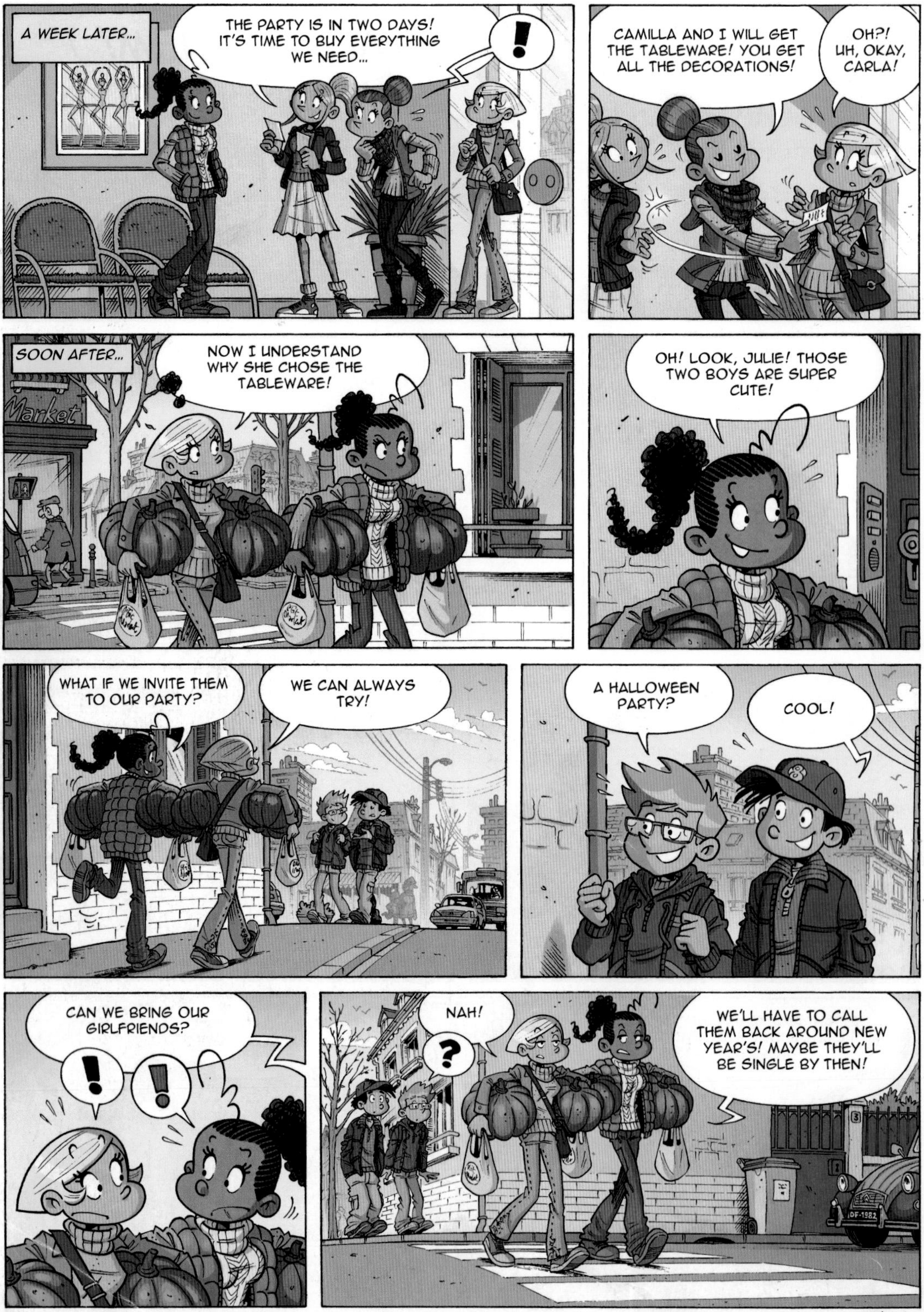
A WEEK LATER...
THE PARTY IS IN TWO DAYS! IT'S TIME TO BUY EVERYTHING WE NEED...
!
CAMILLA AND I WILL GET THE TABLEWARE! YOU GET ALL THE DECORATIONS!
OH?! UH, OKAY, CARLA!
SOON AFTER...
NOW I UNDERSTAND WHY SHE CHOSE THE TABLEWARE!
Market
OH! LOOK, JULIE! THOSE TWO BOYS ARE SUPER CUTE!
WHAT IF WE INVITE THEM TO OUR PARTY?
WE CAN ALWAYS TRY!
A HALLOWEEN PARTY?
COOL!
CAN WE BRING OUR GIRLFRIENDS?
!
!
NAH!
?
WE'LL HAVE TO CALL THEM BACK AROUND NEW YEAR'S! MAYBE THEY'LL BE SINGLE BY THEN!
DF-1982

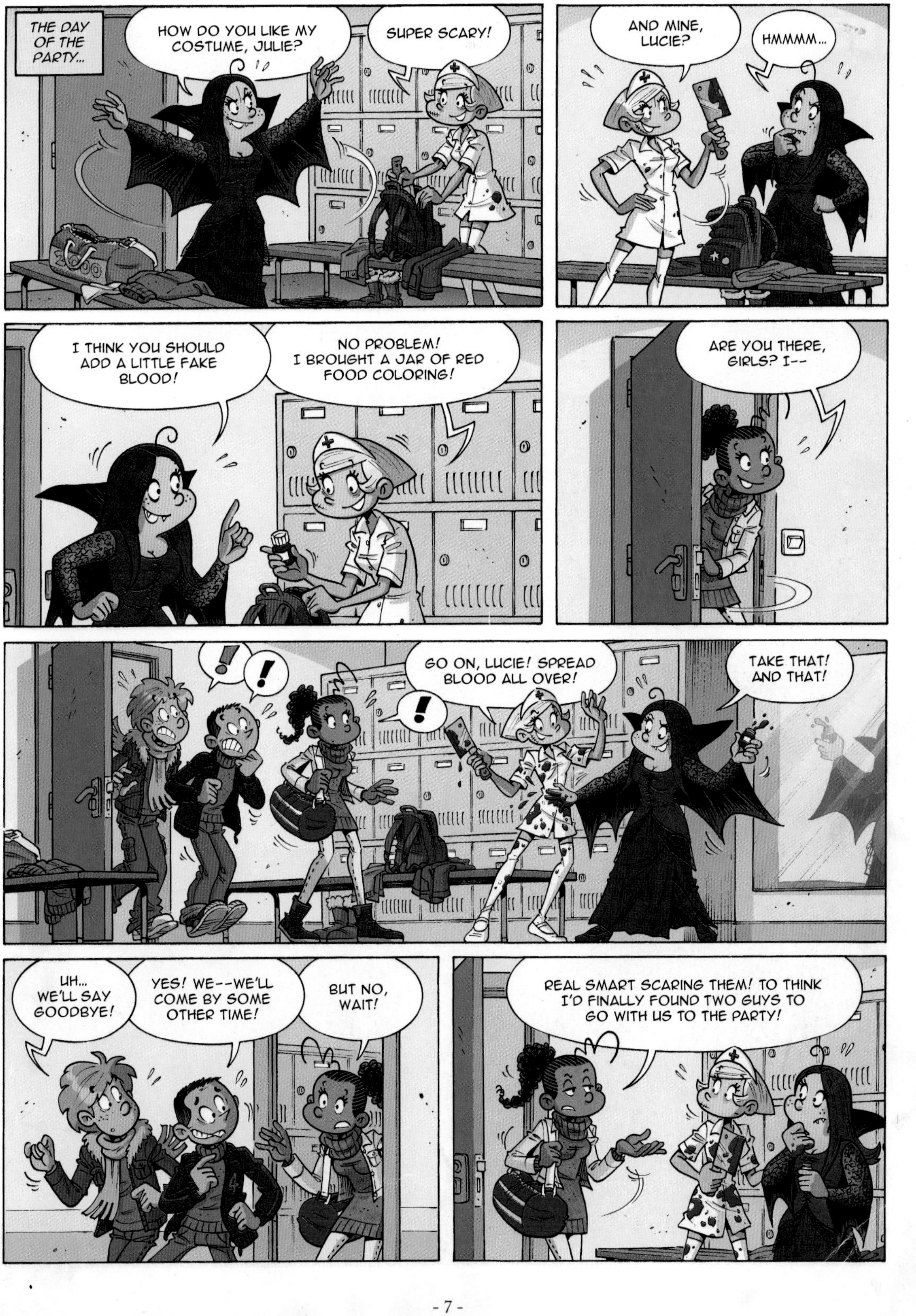

THE DAY OF THE PARTY...
HOW DO YOU LIKE MY COSTUME, JULIE?
SUPER SCARY!
AND MINE, LUCIE?
HMMMM...
I THINK YOU SHOULD ADD A LITTLE FAKE BLOOD!
NO PROBLEM! I BROUGHT A JAR OF RED FOOD COLORING!
ARE YOU THERE, GIRLS? I--
!
!
!
GO ON, LUCIE! SPREAD BLOOD ALL OVER!
TAKE THAT! AND THAT!
UH... WE'LL SAY GOODBYE!
YES! WE--WE'LL COME BY SOME OTHER TIME!
BUT NO, WAIT!
REAL SMART SCARING THEM! TO THINK I'D FINALLY FOUND TWO GUYS TO GO WITH US TO THE PARTY!

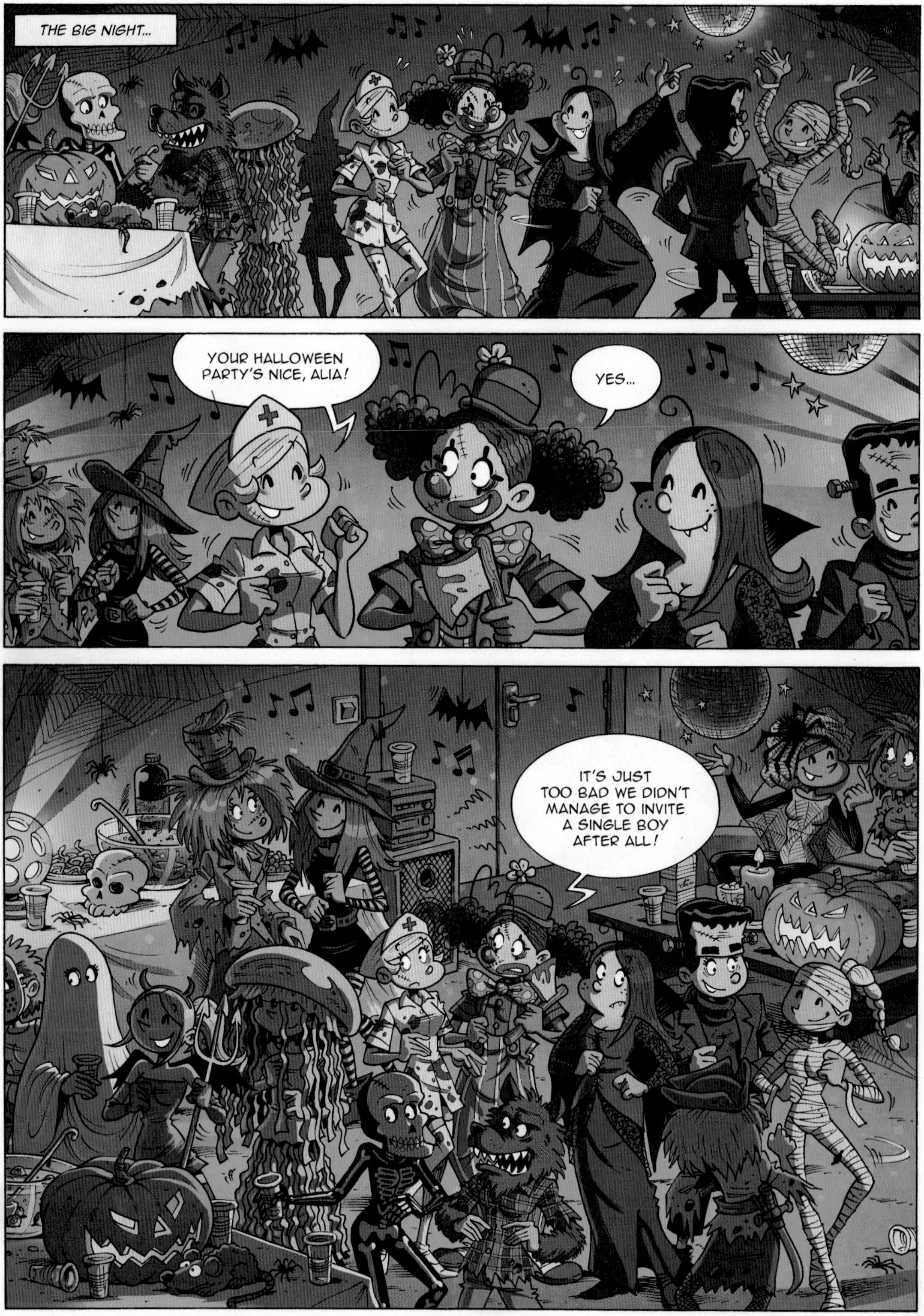

THE BIG NIGHT...
YOUR HALLOWEEN PARTY'S NICE, ALIA!
YES...
IT'S JUST TOO BAD WE DIDN'T MANAGE TO INVITE A SINGLE BOY AFTER ALL!

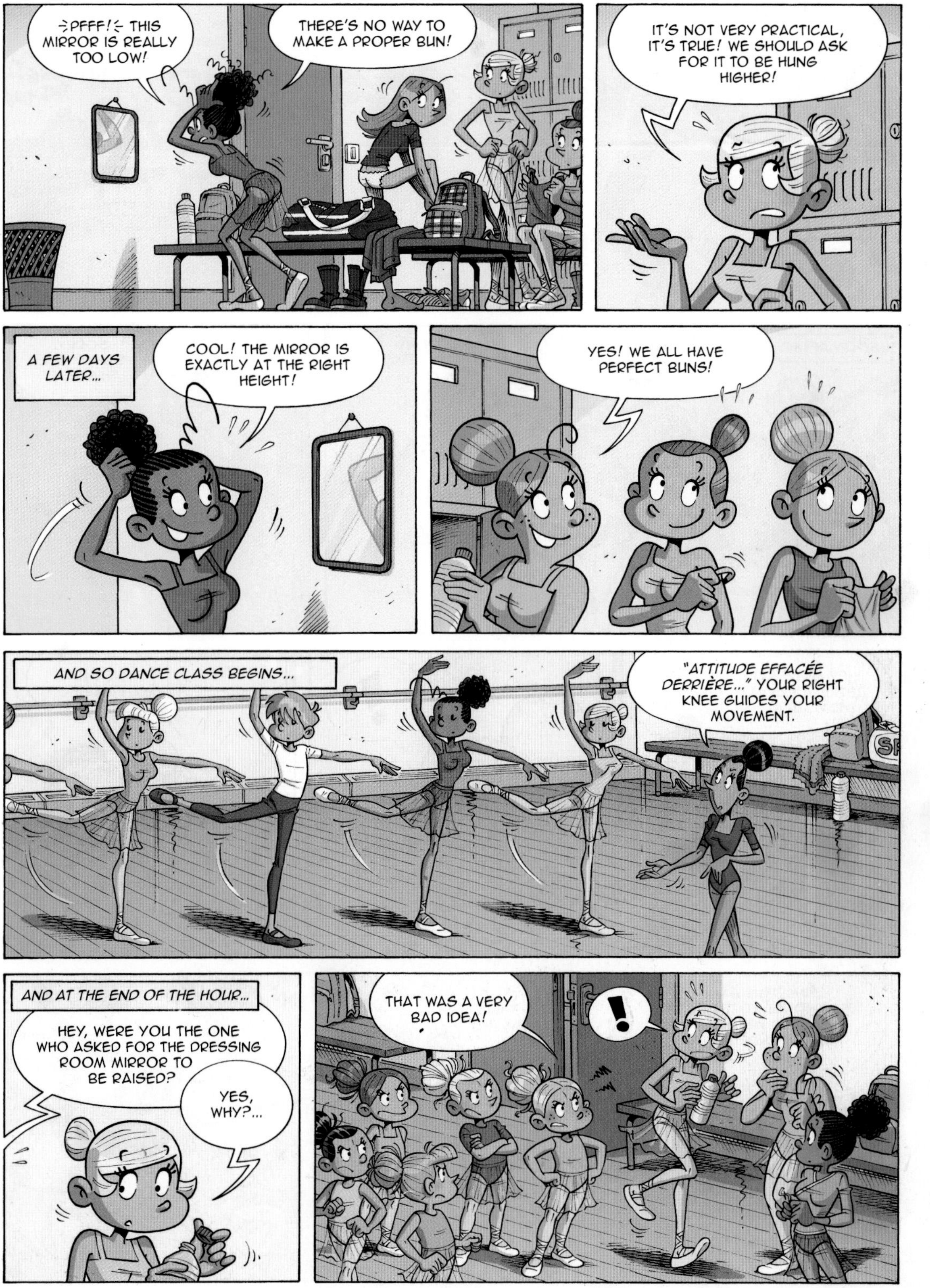

PFFF! THIS MIRROR IS REALLY TOO LOW!
THERE'S NO WAY TO MAKE A PROPER BUN!
IT'S NOT VERY PRACTICAL, IT'S TRUE! WE SHOULD ASK FOR IT TO BE HUNG HIGHER!
A FEW DAYS LATER...
COOL! THE MIRROR IS EXACTLY AT THE RIGHT HEIGHT!
YES! WE ALL HAVE PERFECT BUNS!
AND SO DANCE CLASS BEGINS...
"ATTITUDE EFFACÉE DERRIÈRE..." YOUR RIGHT KNEE GUIDES YOUR MOVEMENT.
AND AT THE END OF THE HOUR...
HEY, WERE YOU THE ONE WHO ASKED FOR THE DRESSING ROOM MIRROR TO BE RAISED?
YES, WHY?...
THAT WAS A VERY BAD IDEA!
!

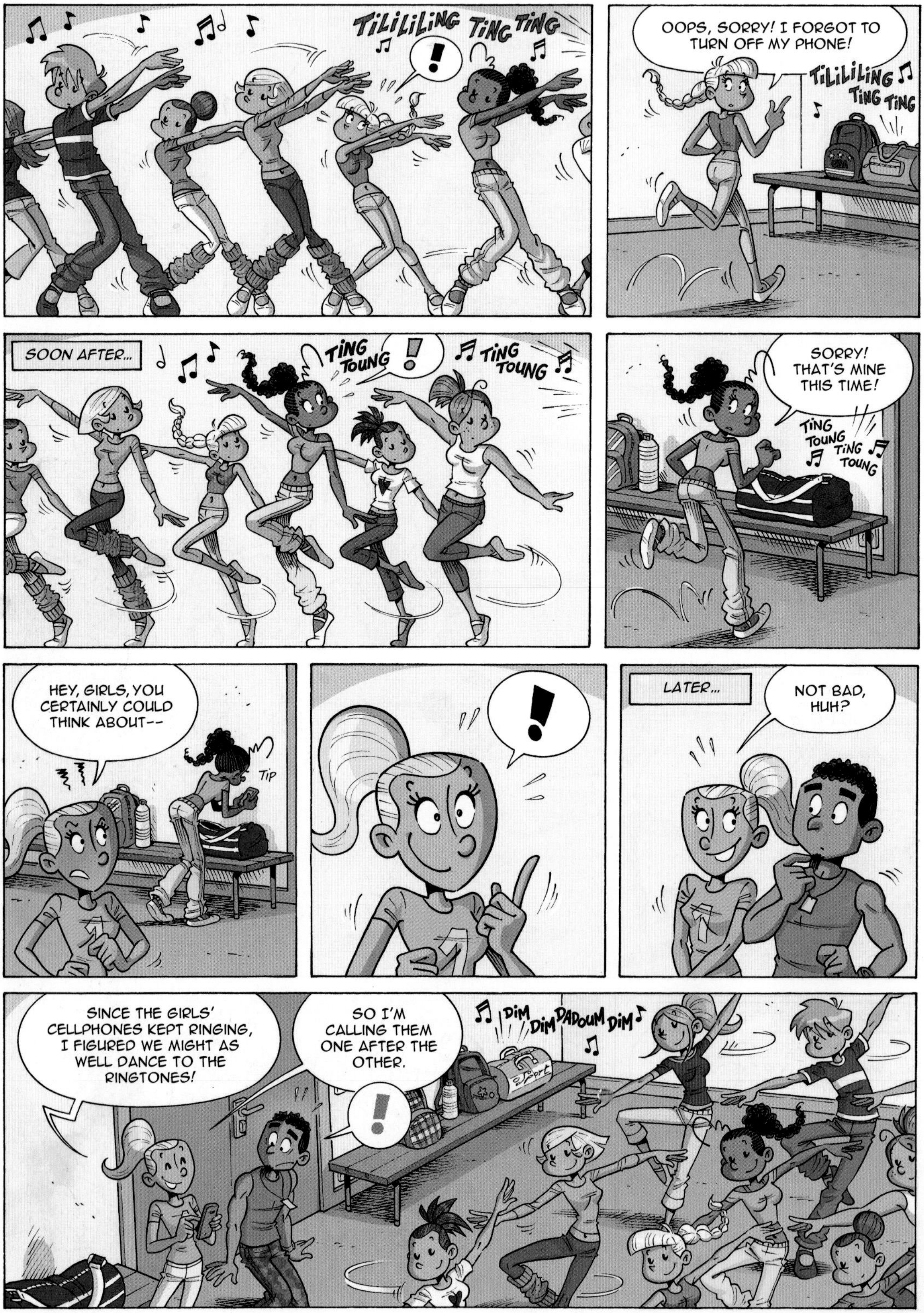
TILILILING TING TING
!
OOPS, SORRY! I FORGOT TO TURN OFF MY PHONE!
TILILILING TING TING
SOON AFTER...
TING TOUNG
!
TING TOUNG
SORRY! THAT'S MINE THIS TIME!
TING TOUNG TING TOUNG
HEY, GIRLS, YOU CERTAINLY COULD THINK ABOUT--
TIP
!
LATER...
NOT BAD, HUH?
SINCE THE GIRLS' CELLPHONES KEPT RINGING, I FIGURED WE MIGHT AS WELL DANCE TO THE RINGTONES!
SO I'M CALLING THEM ONE AFTER THE OTHER.
DIM DIM DADOUM DIM
!

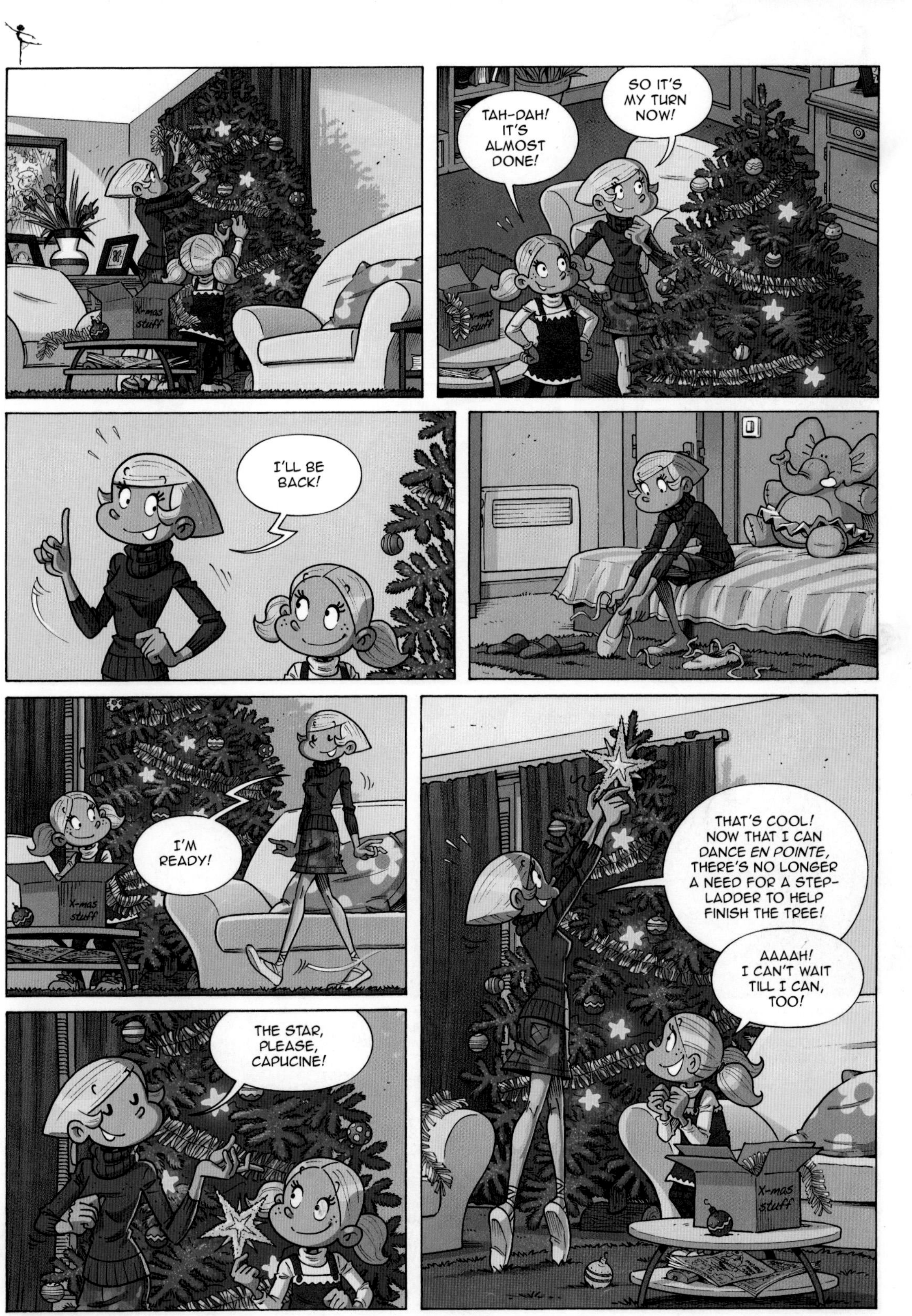

TAH-DAH! IT'S ALMOST DONE!
SO IT'S MY TURN NOW!
I'LL BE BACK!
I'M READY!
THE STAR, PLEASE, CAPUCINE!
THAT'S COOL! NOW THAT I CAN DANCE *EN POINTE*, THERE'S NO LONGER A NEED FOR A STEP-LADDER TO HELP FINISH THE TREE!
AAAAH! I CAN'T WAIT TILL I CAN, TOO!

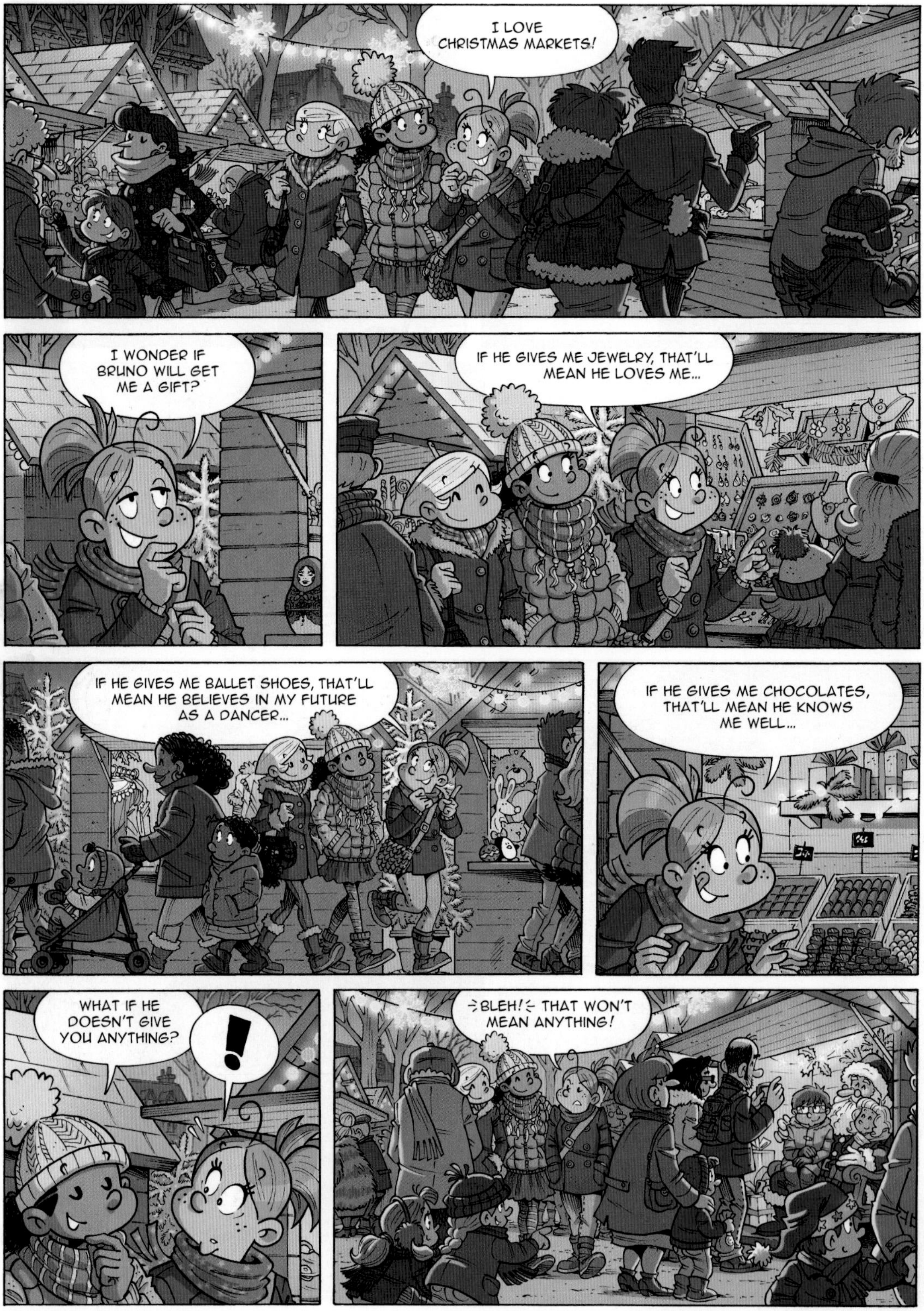
I LOVE CHRISTMAS MARKETS!
I WONDER IF BRUNO WILL GET ME A GIFT?
IF HE GIVES ME JEWELRY, THAT'LL MEAN HE LOVES ME...
IF HE GIVES ME BALLET SHOES, THAT'LL MEAN HE BELIEVES IN MY FUTURE AS A DANCER...
IF HE GIVES ME CHOCOLATES, THAT'LL MEAN HE KNOWS ME WELL...
WHAT IF HE DOESN'T GIVE YOU ANYTHING?
!
BLEH! THAT WON'T MEAN ANYTHING!

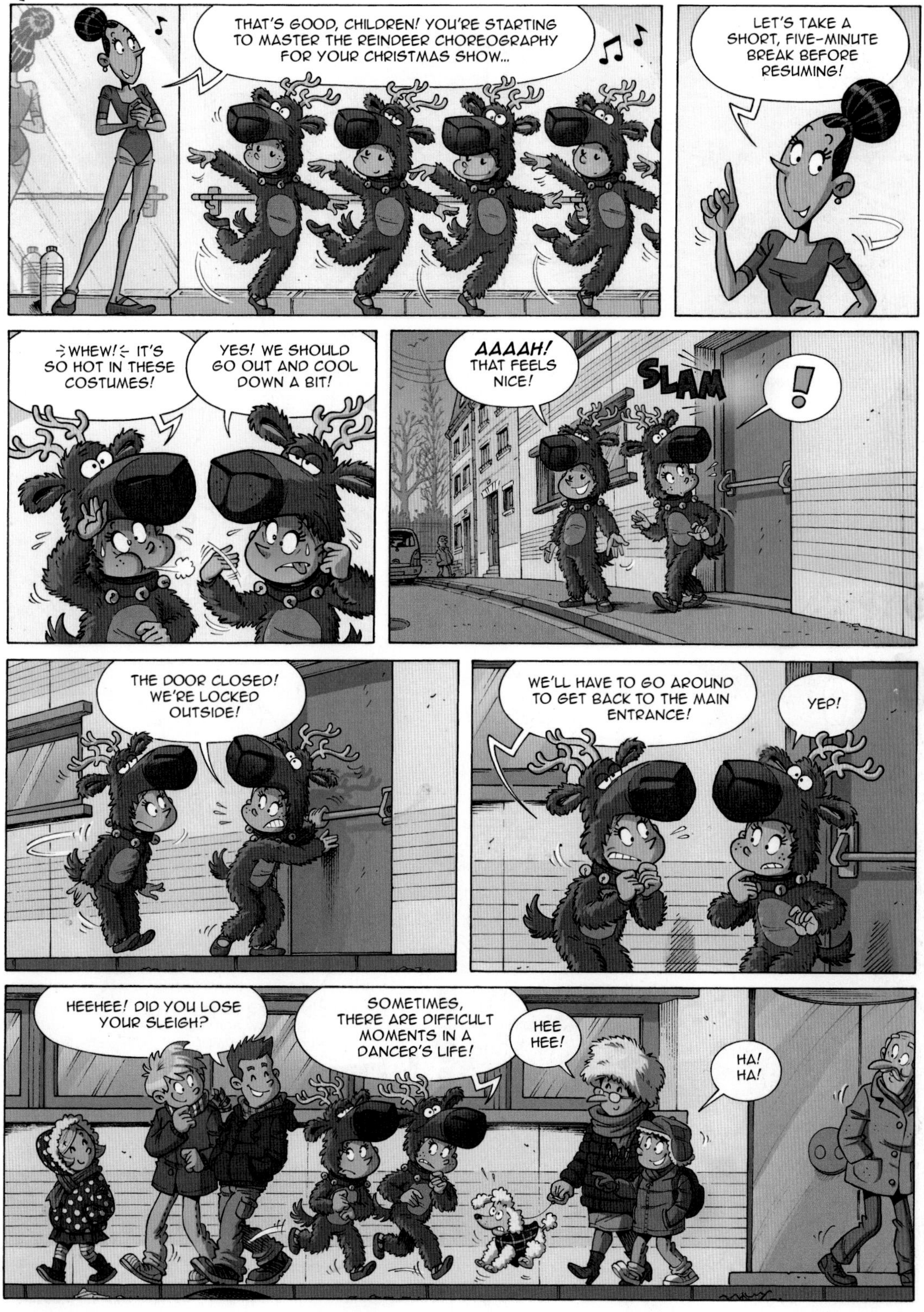

THAT'S GOOD, CHILDREN! YOU'RE STARTING TO MASTER THE REINDEER CHOREOGRAPHY FOR YOUR CHRISTMAS SHOW...
LET'S TAKE A SHORT, FIVE-MINUTE BREAK BEFORE RESUMING!
WHEW! IT'S SO HOT IN THESE COSTUMES!
YES! WE SHOULD GO OUT AND COOL DOWN A BIT!
AAAAH! THAT FEELS NICE!
SLAM
!
THE DOOR CLOSED! WE'RE LOCKED OUTSIDE!
WE'LL HAVE TO GO AROUND TO GET BACK TO THE MAIN ENTRANCE!
YEP!
HEEHEE! DID YOU LOSE YOUR SLEIGH?
SOMETIMES, THERE ARE DIFFICULT MOMENTS IN A DANCER'S LIFE!
HEE HEE!
HA! HA!

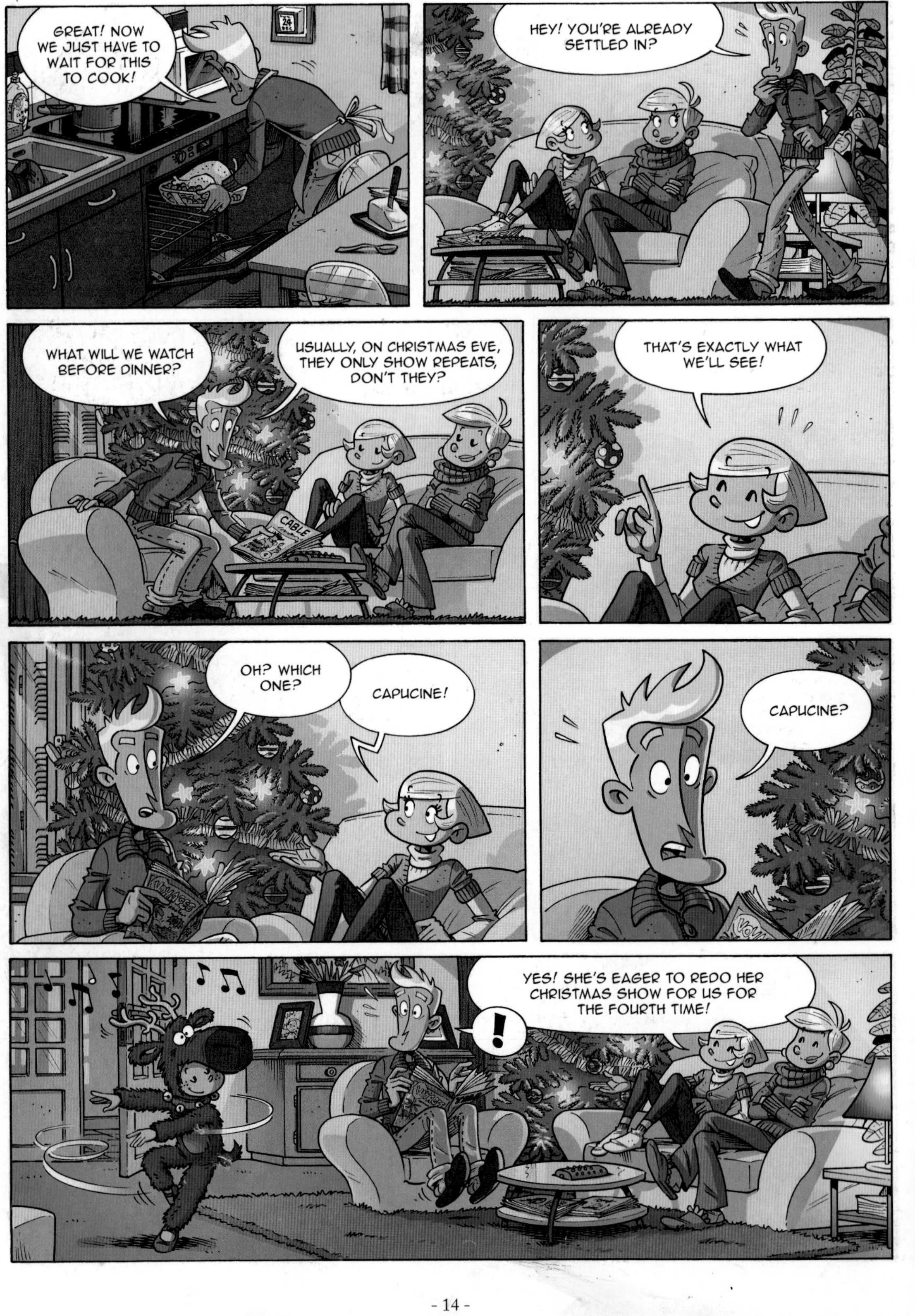
GREAT! NOW WE JUST HAVE TO WAIT FOR THIS TO COOK!
HEY! YOU'RE ALREADY SETTLED IN?
WHAT WILL WE WATCH BEFORE DINNER?
USUALLY, ON CHRISTMAS EVE, THEY ONLY SHOW REPEATS, DON'T THEY?
CABLE
THAT'S EXACTLY WHAT WE'LL SEE!
OH? WHICH ONE?
CAPUCINE!
CAPUCINE?
!
YES! SHE'S EAGER TO REDO HER CHRISTMAS SHOW FOR US FOR THE FOURTH TIME!

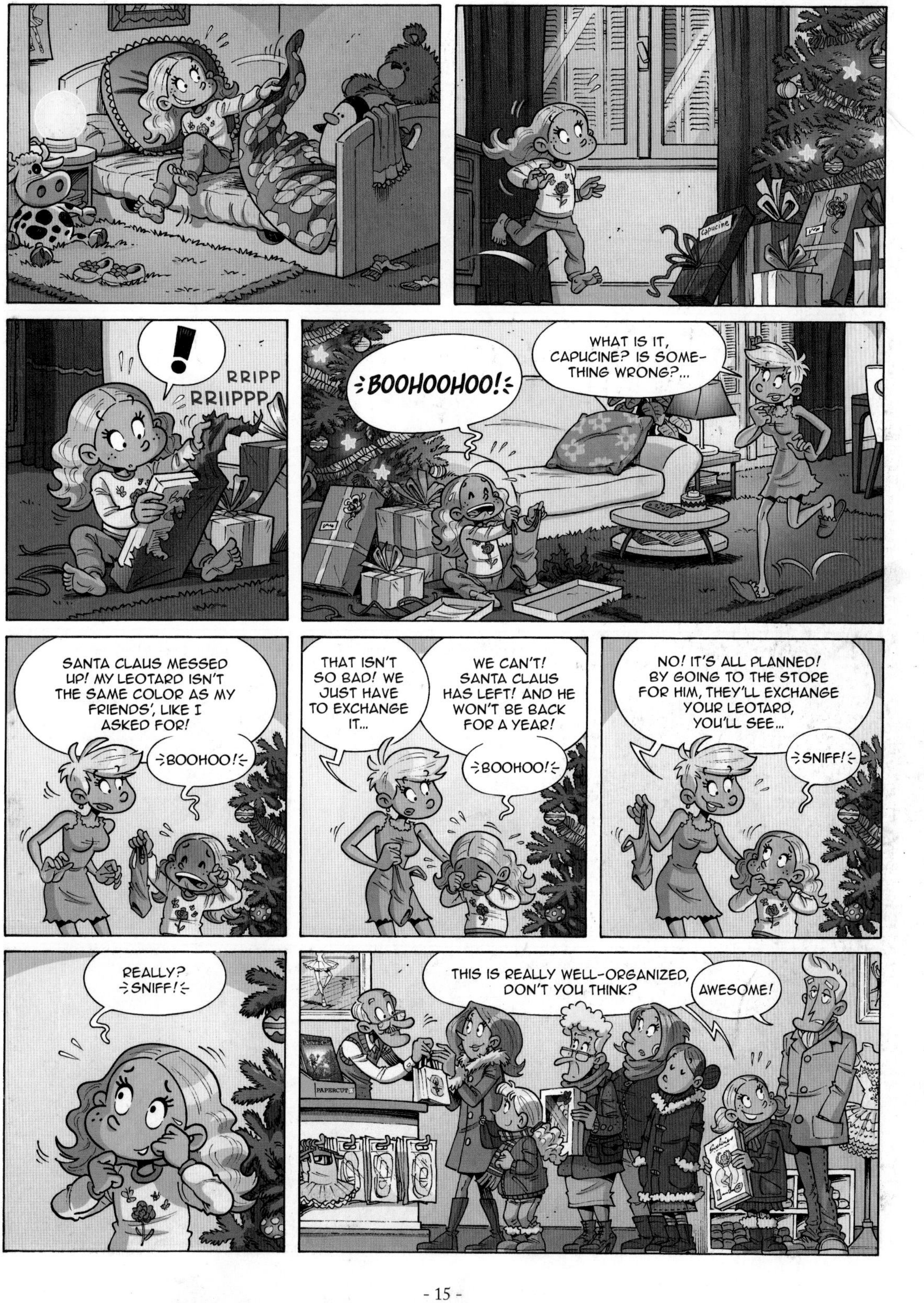
!
RRIPP
RRIIPPP
BOOHOOHOO!
WHAT IS IT, CAPUCINE? IS SOMETHING WRONG?...
SANTA CLAUS MESSED UP! MY LEOTARD ISN'T THE SAME COLOR AS MY FRIENDS', LIKE I ASKED FOR!
BOOHOO!
THAT ISN'T SO BAD! WE JUST HAVE TO EXCHANGE IT...
WE CAN'T! SANTA CLAUS HAS LEFT! AND HE WON'T BE BACK FOR A YEAR!
BOOHOO!
NO! IT'S ALL PLANNED! BY GOING TO THE STORE FOR HIM, THEY'LL EXCHANGE YOUR LEOTARD, YOU'LL SEE...
SNIFF!
REALLY? SNIFF!
THIS IS REALLY WELL-ORGANIZED, DON'T YOU THINK?
AWESOME!

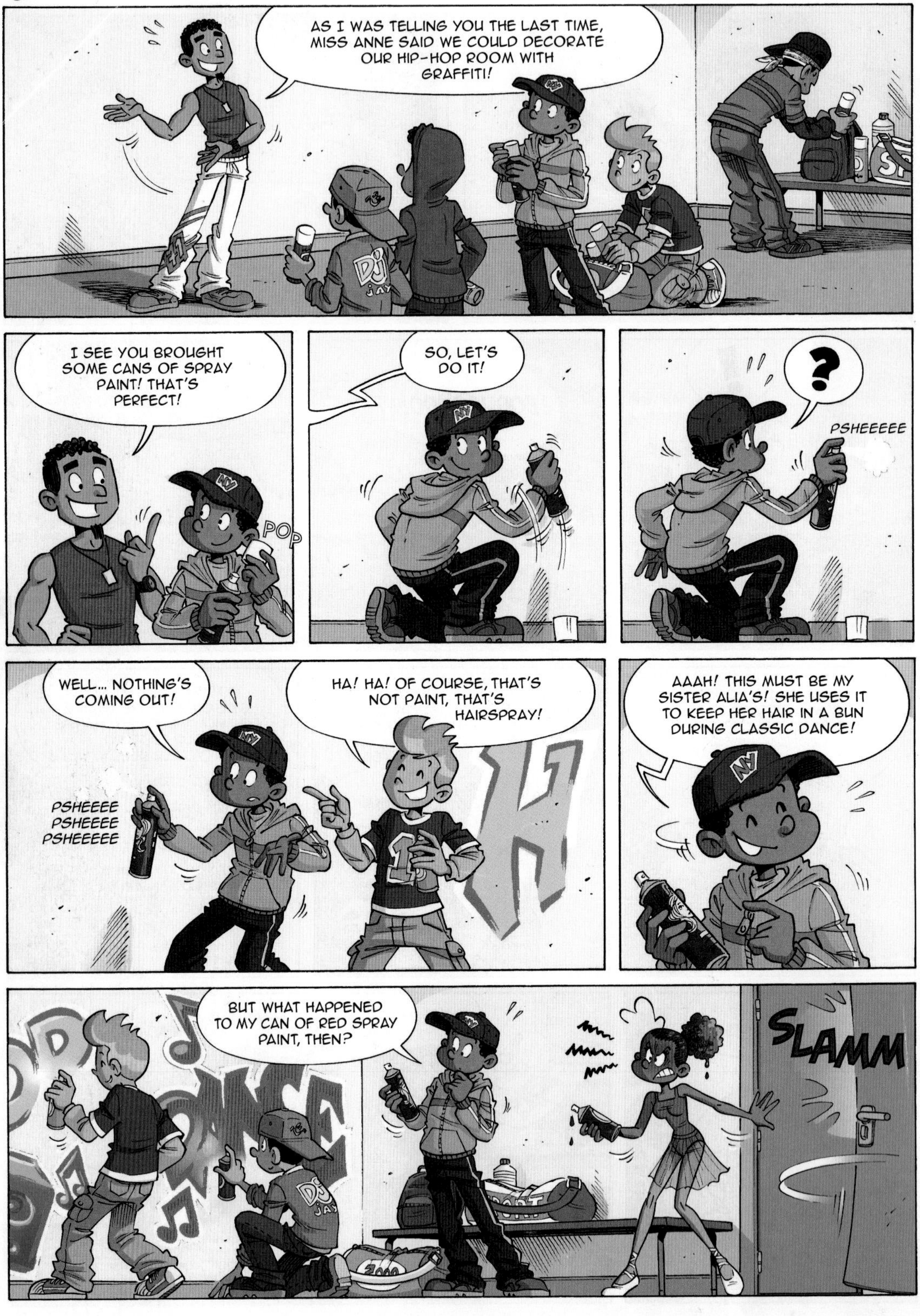
AS I WAS TELLING YOU THE LAST TIME, MISS ANNE SAID WE COULD DECORATE OUR HIP-HOP ROOM WITH GRAFFITI!
I SEE YOU BROUGHT SOME CANS OF SPRAY PAINT! THAT'S PERFECT!
POP
SO, LET'S DO IT!
?
PSHEEEEE
WELL... NOTHING'S COMING OUT!
PSHEEEE
PSHEEEE
PSHEEEEE
HA! HA! OF COURSE, THAT'S NOT PAINT, THAT'S HAIRSPRAY!
AAAH! THIS MUST BE MY SISTER ALIA'S! SHE USES IT TO KEEP HER HAIR IN A BUN DURING CLASSIC DANCE!
BUT WHAT HAPPENED TO MY CAN OF RED SPRAY PAINT, THEN?
SLAMM

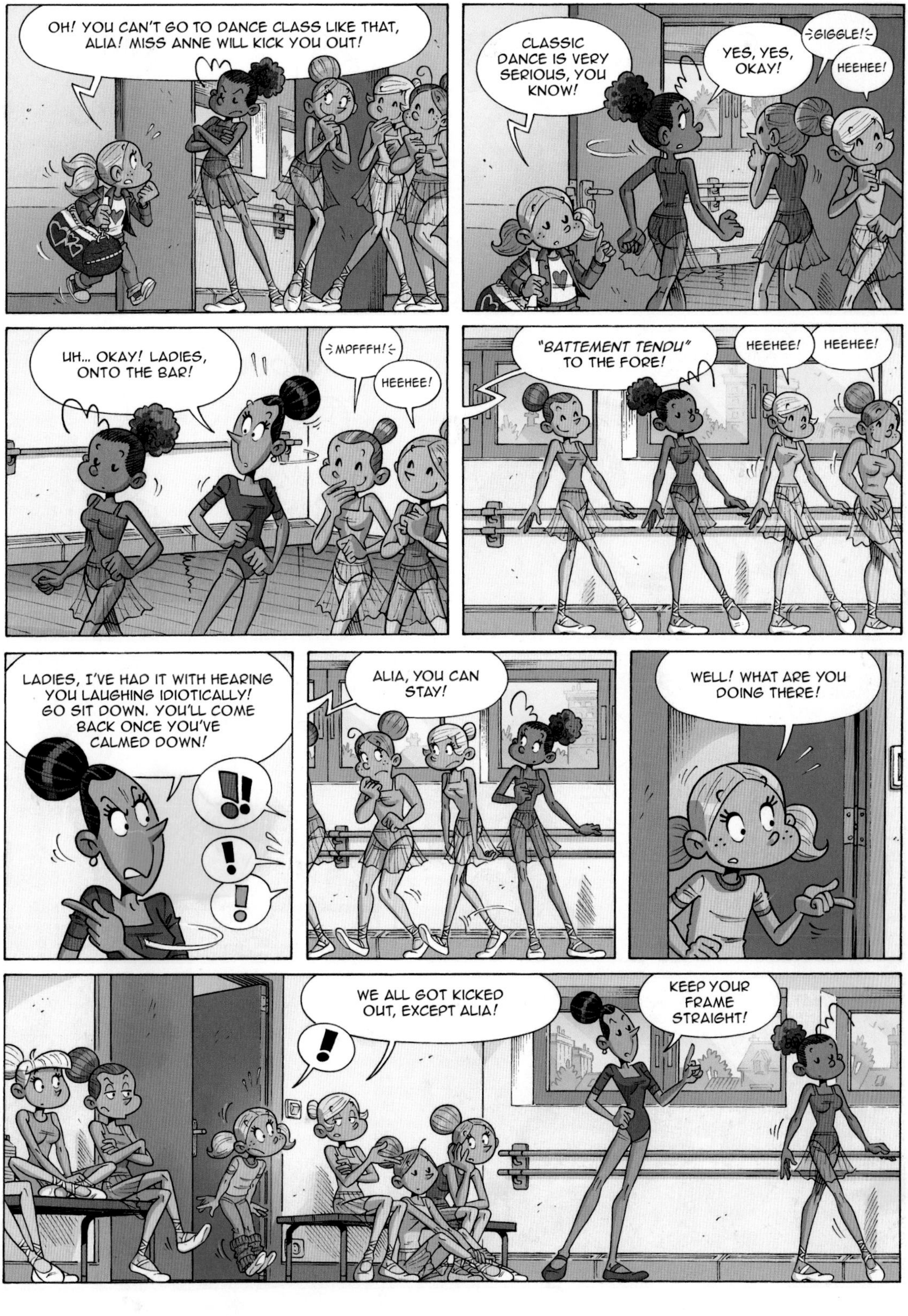

OH! YOU CAN'T GO TO DANCE CLASS LIKE THAT, ALIA! MISS ANNE WILL KICK YOU OUT!
CLASSIC DANCE IS VERY SERIOUS, YOU KNOW!
YES, YES, OKAY!
GIGGLE!
HEEHEE!
UH... OKAY! LADIES, ONTO THE BAR!
MPFFFH!
HEEHEE!
"BATTEMENT TENDU" TO THE FORE!
HEEHEE!
HEEHEE!
LADIES, I'VE HAD IT WITH HEARING YOU LAUGHING IDIOTICALLY! GO SIT DOWN. YOU'LL COME BACK ONCE YOU'VE CALMED DOWN!
!!
!
!
ALIA, YOU CAN STAY!
WELL! WHAT ARE YOU DOING THERE!
!
WE ALL GOT KICKED OUT, EXCEPT ALIA!
KEEP YOUR FRAME STRAIGHT!

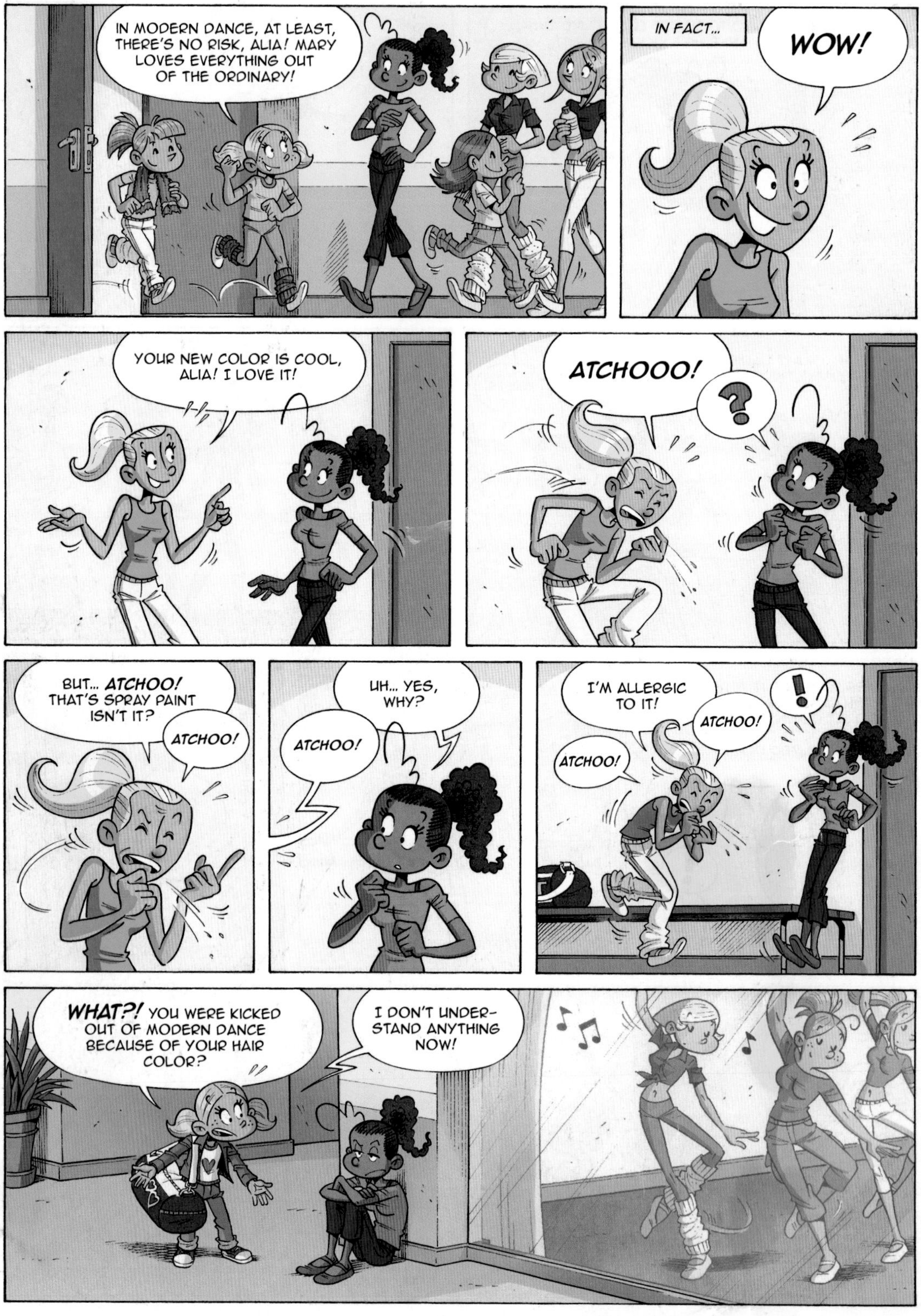
IN MODERN DANCE, AT LEAST, THERE'S NO RISK, ALIA! MARY LOVES EVERYTHING OUT OF THE ORDINARY!
IN FACT...
WOW!
YOUR NEW COLOR IS COOL, ALIA! I LOVE IT!
ATCHOOO!
?
BUT... ATCHOO! THAT'S SPRAY PAINT ISN'T IT?
ATCHOO!
UH... YES, WHY?
ATCHOO!
I'M ALLERGIC TO IT!
ATCHOO!
ATCHOO!
!
WHAT?! YOU WERE KICKED OUT OF MODERN DANCE BECAUSE OF YOUR HAIR COLOR?
I DON'T UNDER-STAND ANYTHING NOW!

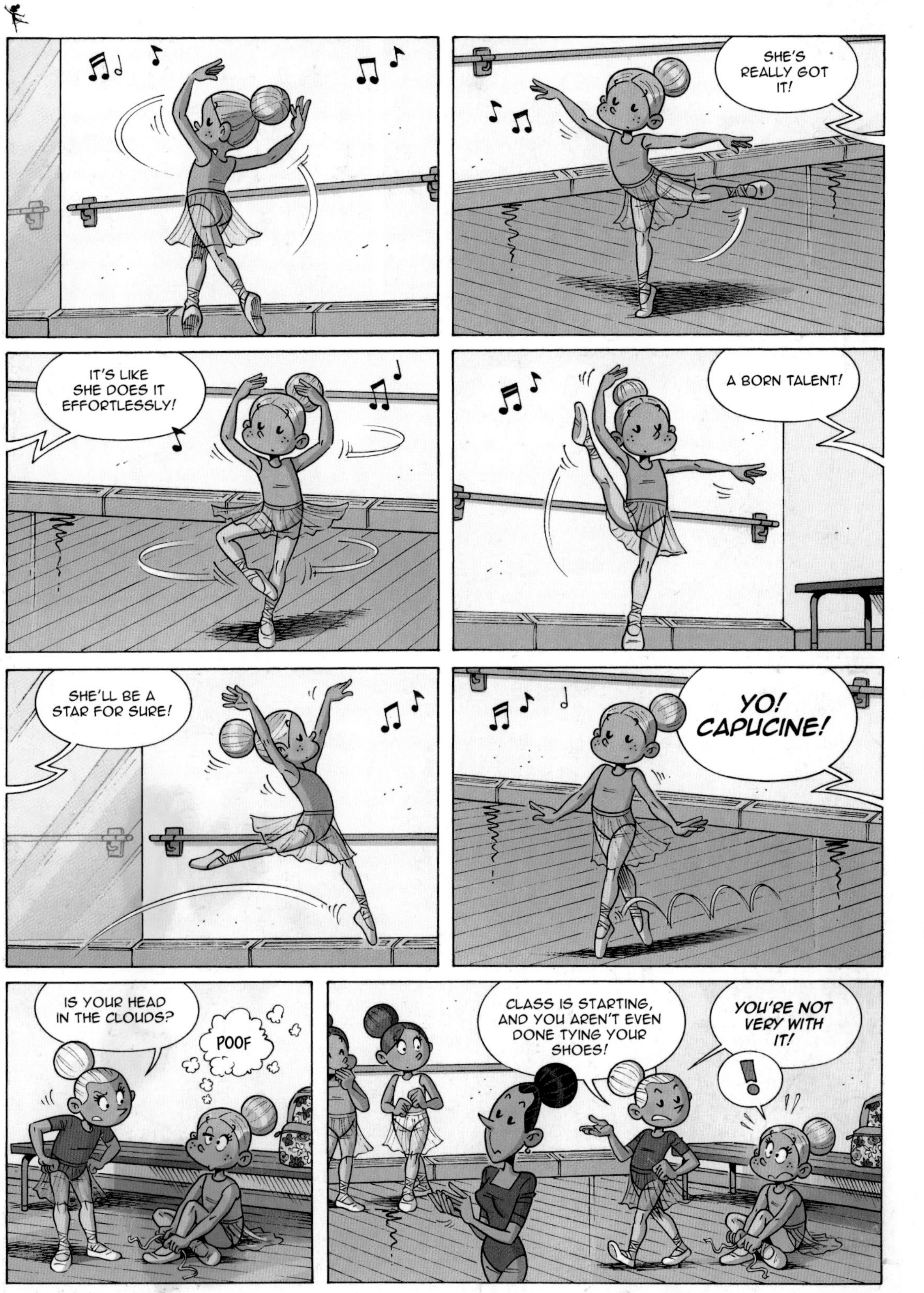
SHE'S REALLY GOT IT!
IT'S LIKE SHE DOES IT EFFORTLESSLY!
A BORN TALENT!
SHE'LL BE A STAR FOR SURE!
YO! CAPUCINE!
IS YOUR HEAD IN THE CLOUDS?
POOF
CLASS IS STARTING, AND YOU AREN'T EVEN DONE TYING YOUR SHOES!
YOU'RE NOT VERY WITH IT!
!

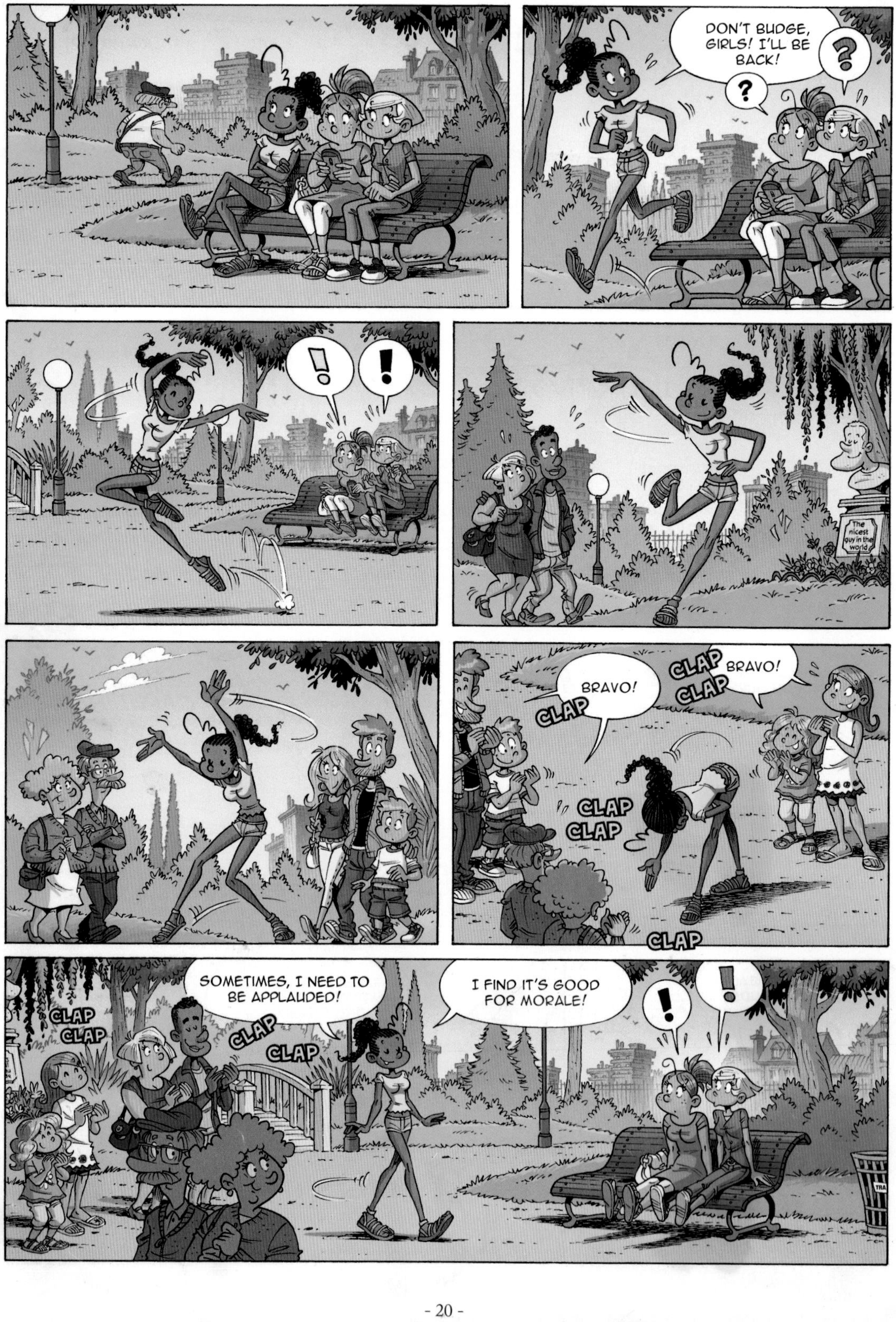
DON'T BUDGE, GIRLS! I'LL BE BACK!
?
?
!
!
The nicest guy in the world
CLAP
BRAVO!
CLAP
CLAP
BRAVO!
CLAP
CLAP
CLAP
CLAP
CLAP
SOMETIMES, I NEED TO BE APPLAUDED!
CLAP
CLAP
I FIND IT'S GOOD FOR MORALE!
!
!

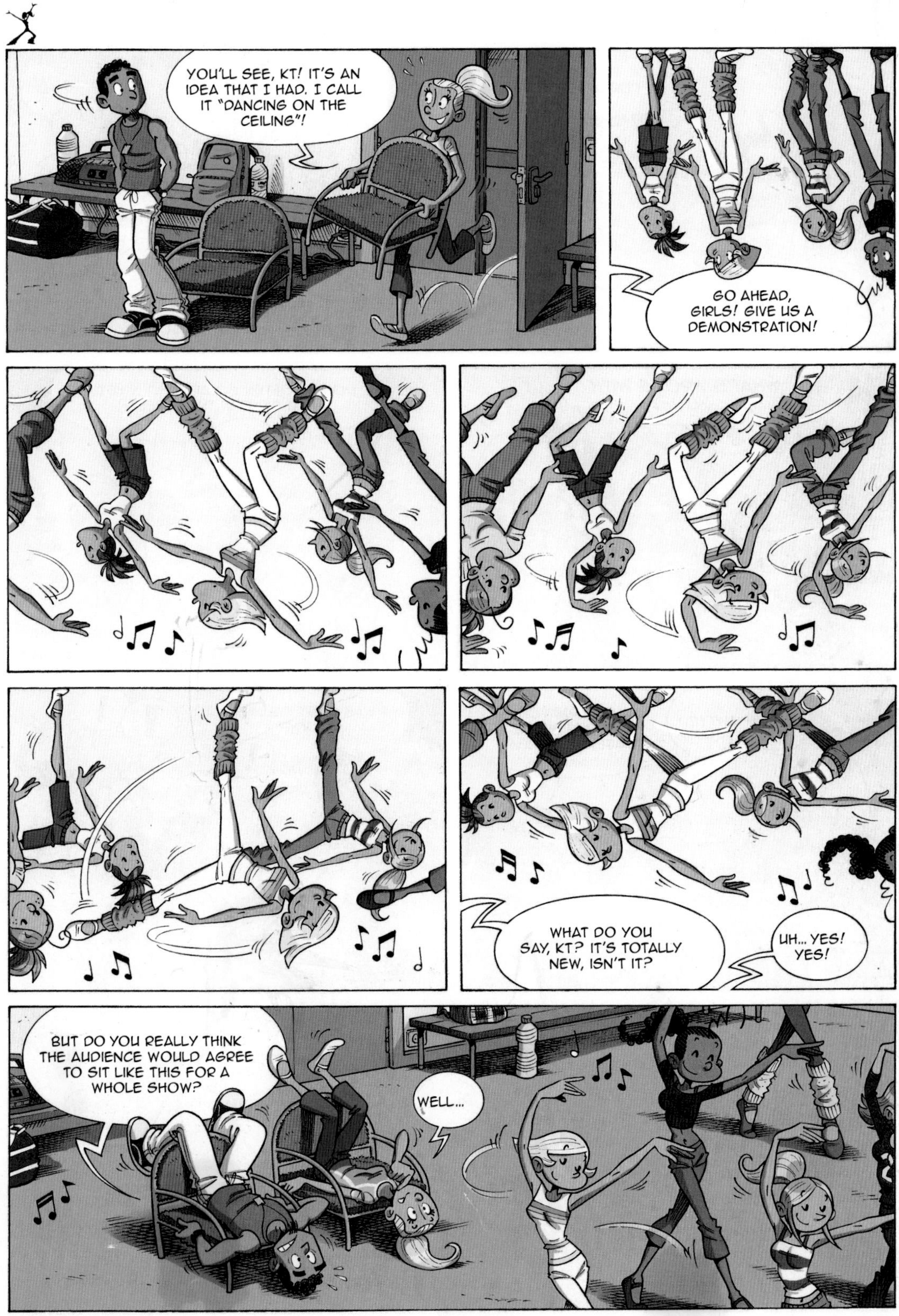
YOU'LL SEE, KT! IT'S AN IDEA THAT I HAD. I CALL IT "DANCING ON THE CEILING"!
GO AHEAD, GIRLS! GIVE US A DEMONSTRATION!
WHAT DO YOU SAY, KT? IT'S TOTALLY NEW, ISN'T IT?
UH... YES! YES!
BUT DO YOU REALLY THINK THE AUDIENCE WOULD AGREE TO SIT LIKE THIS FOR A WHOLE SHOW?
WELL...

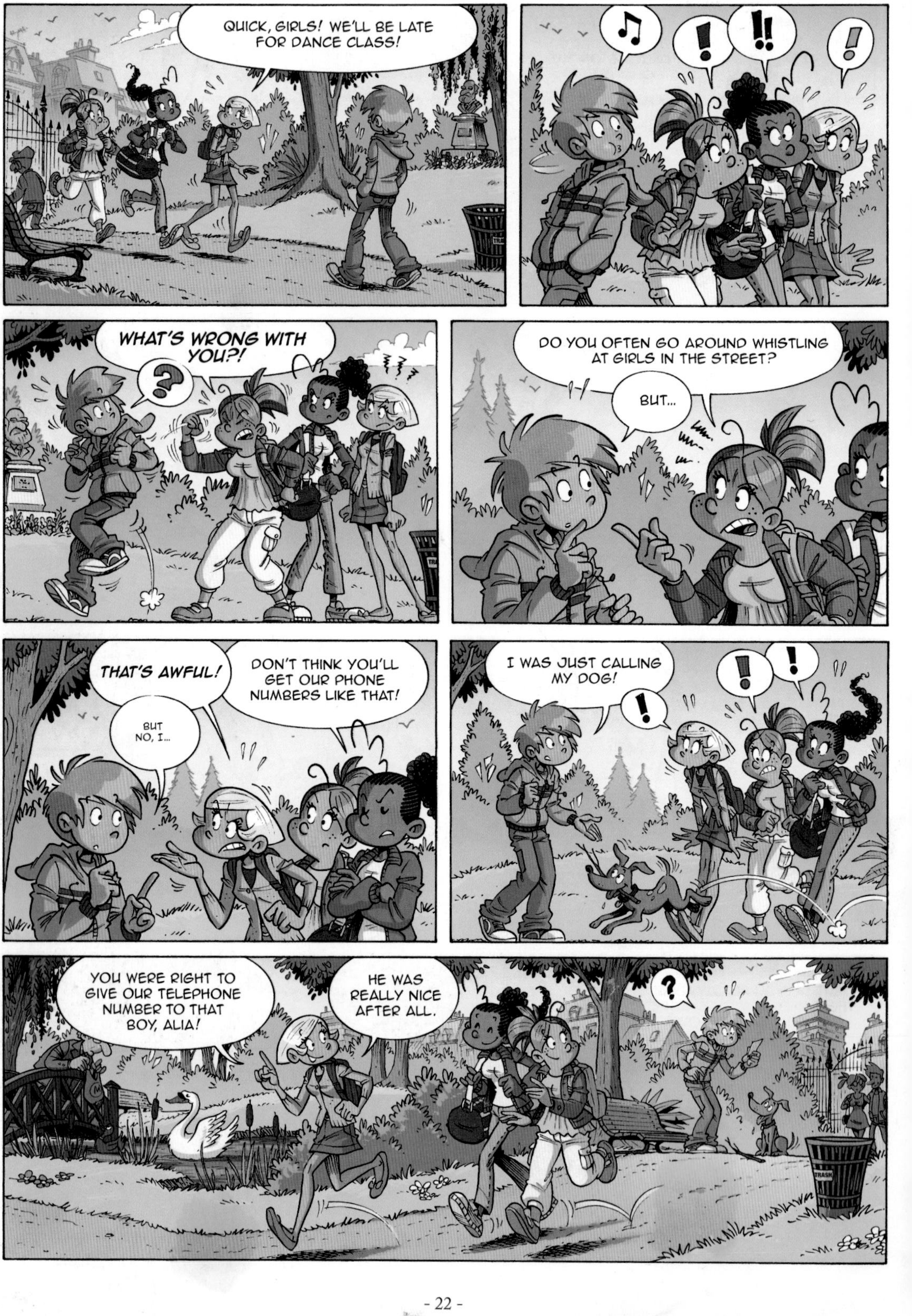
QUICK, GIRLS! WE'LL BE LATE FOR DANCE CLASS!
♪
!
!!
!
WHAT'S WRONG WITH YOU?!
?
DO YOU OFTEN GO AROUND WHISTLING AT GIRLS IN THE STREET?
BUT...
THAT'S AWFUL!
BUT NO, I...
DON'T THINK YOU'LL GET OUR PHONE NUMBERS LIKE THAT!
I WAS JUST CALLING MY DOG!
!
!
!
YOU WERE RIGHT TO GIVE OUR TELEPHONE NUMBER TO THAT BOY, ALIA!
HE WAS REALLY NICE AFTER ALL.
?

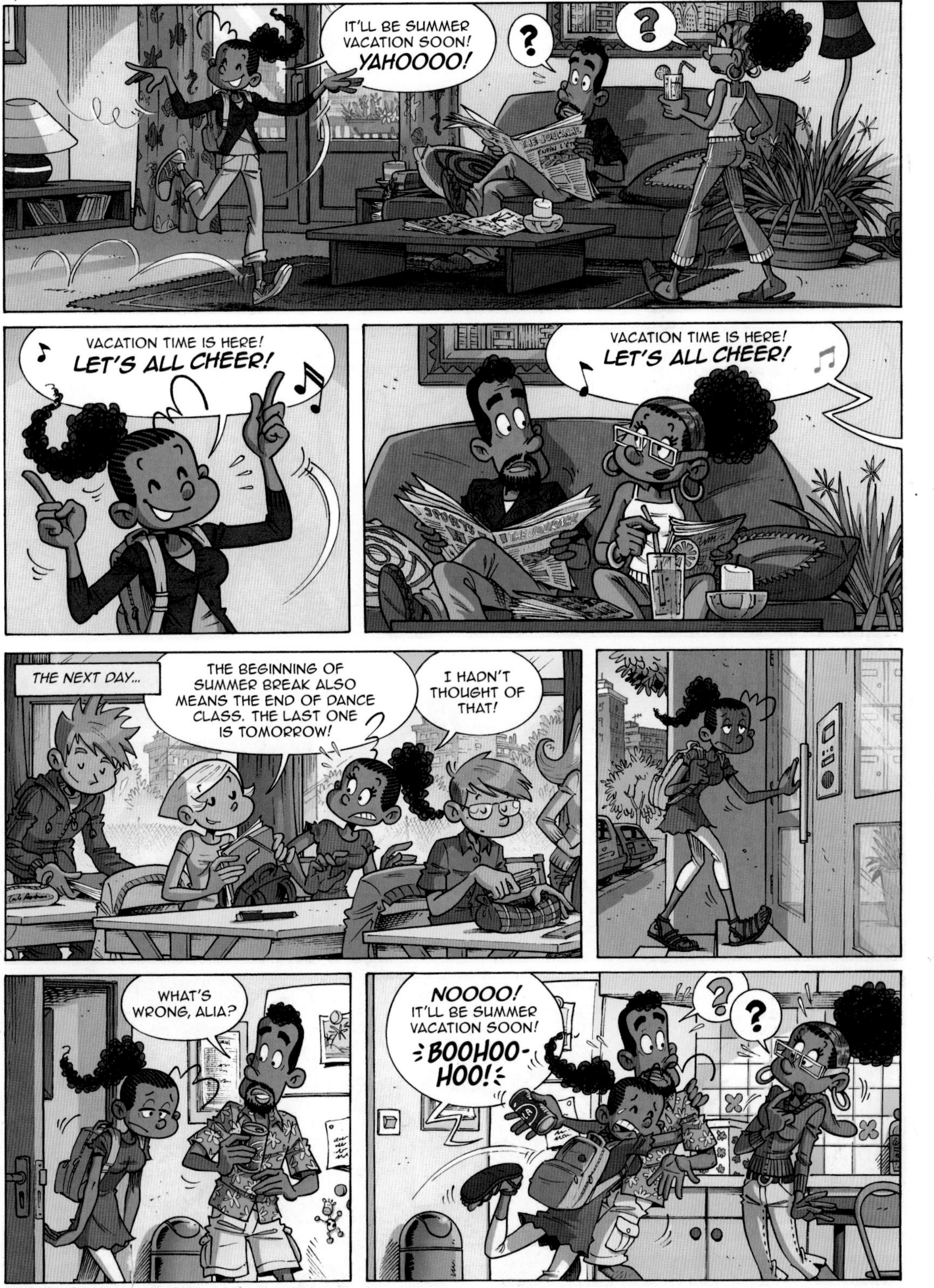

IT'LL BE SUMMER VACATION SOON! YAHOOOO!
?
?
THE JOURNAL
VACATION TIME IS HERE! LET'S ALL CHEER!
VACATION TIME IS HERE! LET'S ALL CHEER!
THE NEXT DAY...
THE BEGINNING OF SUMMER BREAK ALSO MEANS THE END OF DANCE CLASS. THE LAST ONE IS TOMORROW!
I HADN'T THOUGHT OF THAT!
WHAT'S WRONG, ALIA?
NOOOO! IT'LL BE SUMMER VACATION SOON! BOOHOO-HOO!
?
?

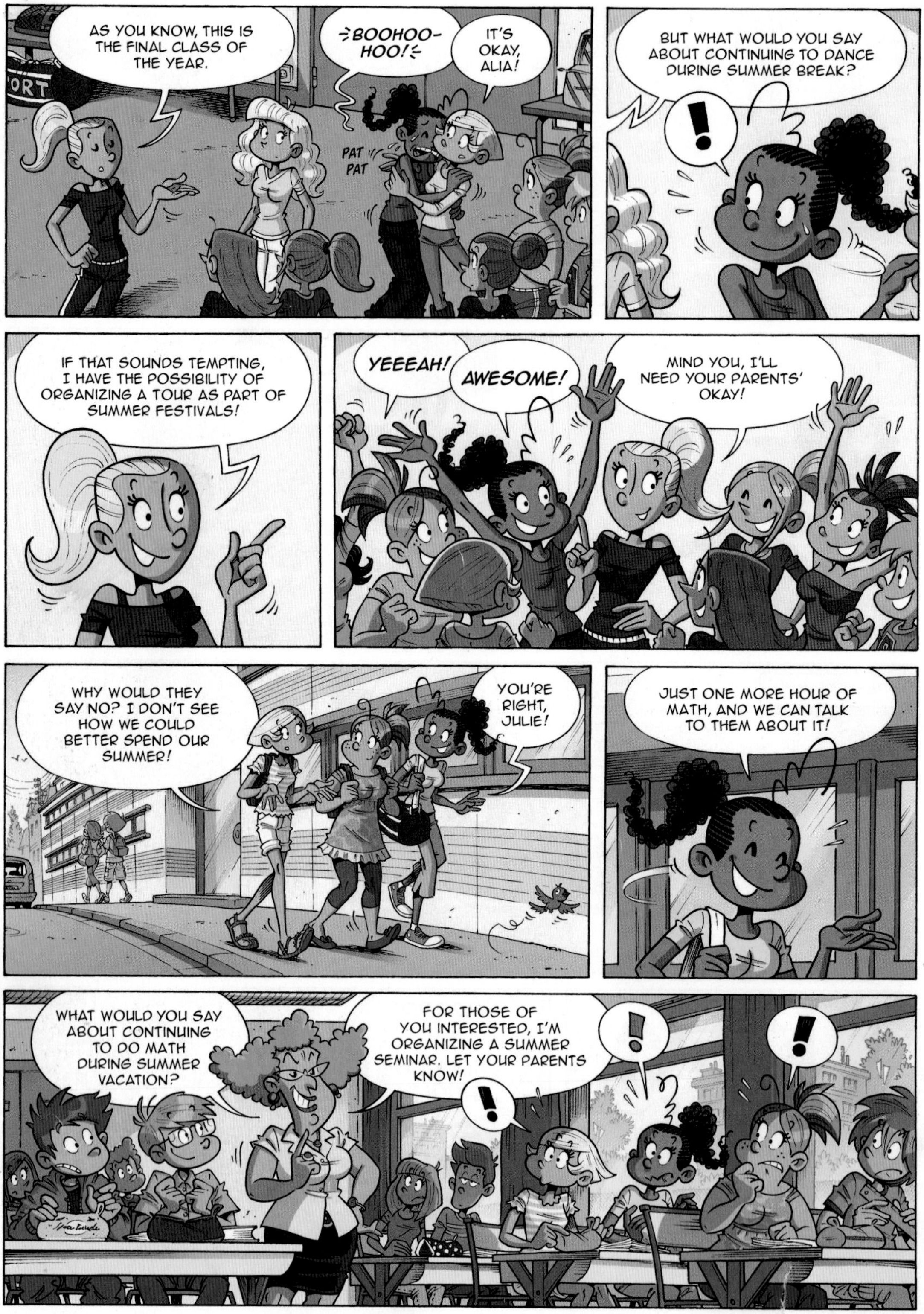
AS YOU KNOW, THIS IS THE FINAL CLASS OF THE YEAR.
BOOHOO-HOO!
IT'S OKAY, ALIA!
PAT PAT
BUT WHAT WOULD YOU SAY ABOUT CONTINUING TO DANCE DURING SUMMER BREAK?
!
IF THAT SOUNDS TEMPTING, I HAVE THE POSSIBILITY OF ORGANIZING A TOUR AS PART OF SUMMER FESTIVALS!
YEEEAH!
AWESOME!
MIND YOU, I'LL NEED YOUR PARENTS' OKAY!
WHY WOULD THEY SAY NO? I DON'T SEE HOW WE COULD BETTER SPEND OUR SUMMER!
YOU'RE RIGHT, JULIE!
JUST ONE MORE HOUR OF MATH, AND WE CAN TALK TO THEM ABOUT IT!
WHAT WOULD YOU SAY ABOUT CONTINUING TO DO MATH DURING SUMMER VACATION?
FOR THOSE OF YOU INTERESTED, I'M ORGANIZING A SUMMER SEMINAR. LET YOUR PARENTS KNOW!
!
!
!

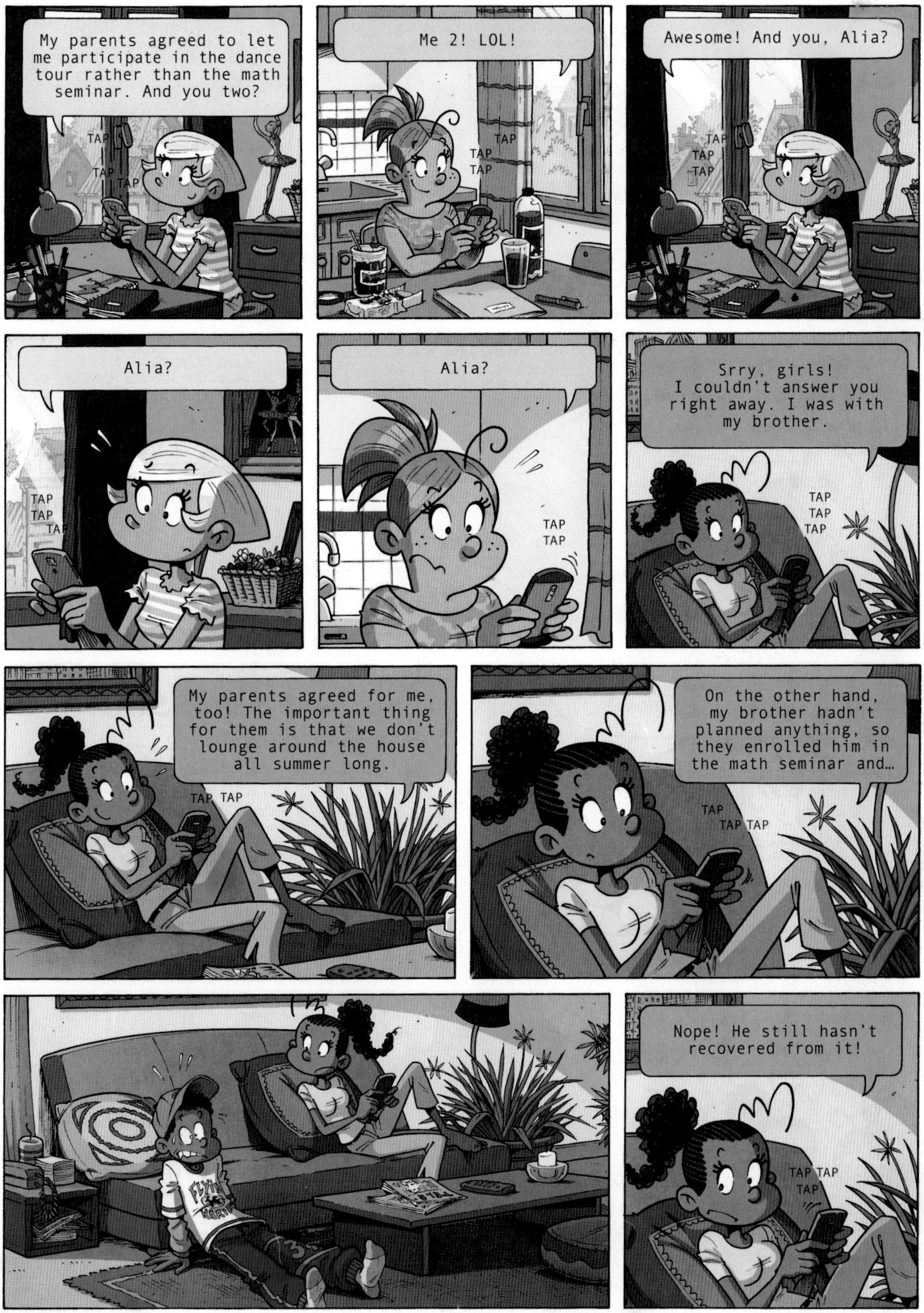
My parents agreed to let me participate in the dance tour rather than the math seminar. And you two?
TAP
TAP TAP
Me 2! LOL!
TAP
TAP
TAP
Awesome! And you, Alia?
TAP
TAP
TAP
Alia?
TAP
TAP
TAP
Alia?
TAP
TAP
Srry, girls! I couldn't answer you right away. I was with my brother.
TAP
TAP
TAP
My parents agreed for me, too! The important thing for them is that we don't lounge around the house all summer long.
TAP TAP
On the other hand, my brother hadn't planned anything, so they enrolled him in the math seminar and...
TAP
TAP TAP
Nope! He still hasn't recovered from it!
TAP TAP
TAP

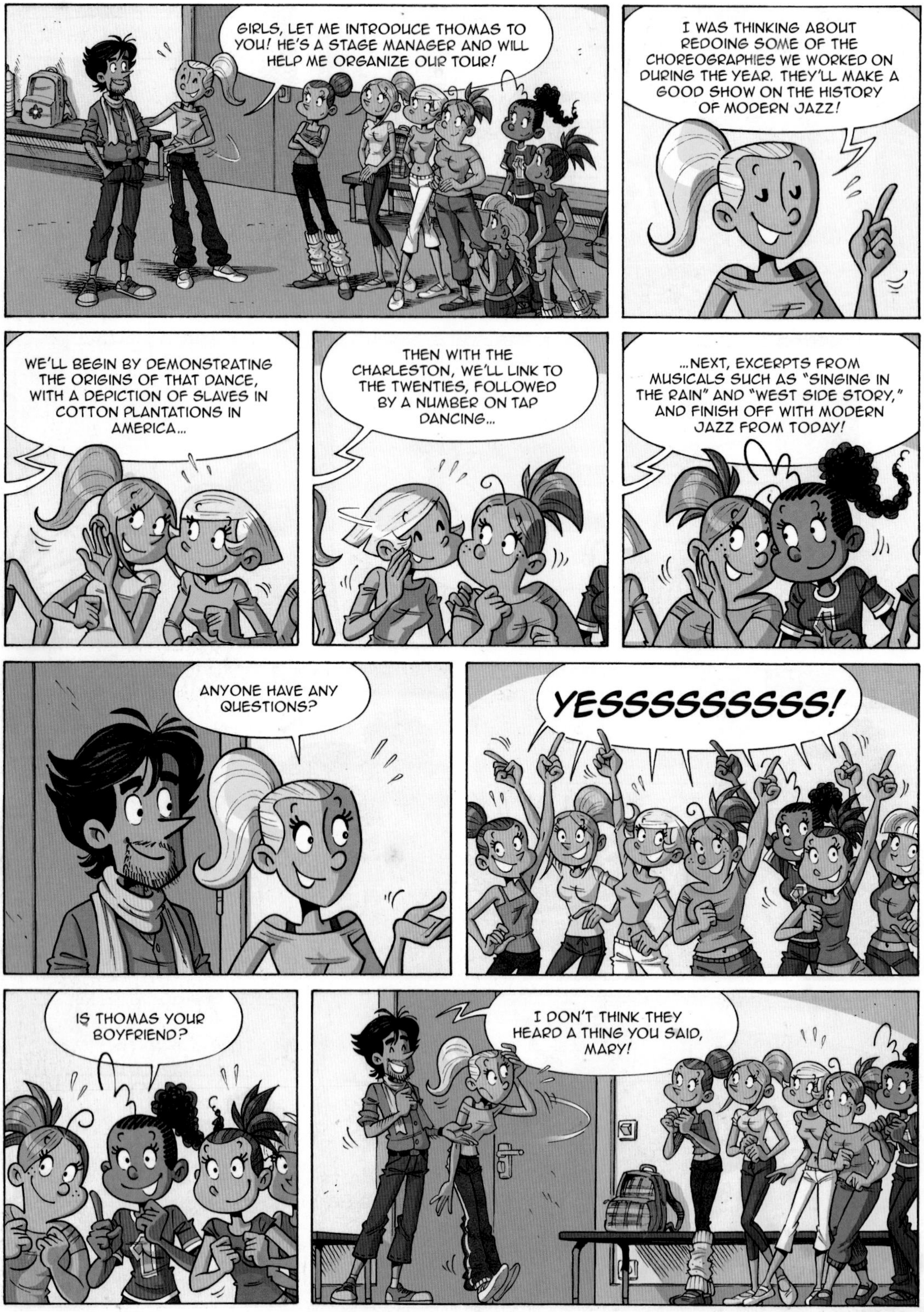
GIRLS, LET ME INTRODUCE THOMAS TO YOU! HE'S A STAGE MANAGER AND WILL HELP ME ORGANIZE OUR TOUR!
I WAS THINKING ABOUT REDOING SOME OF THE CHOREOGRAPHIES WE WORKED ON DURING THE YEAR. THEY'LL MAKE A GOOD SHOW ON THE HISTORY OF MODERN JAZZ!
WE'LL BEGIN BY DEMONSTRATING THE ORIGINS OF THAT DANCE, WITH A DEPICTION OF SLAVES IN COTTON PLANTATIONS IN AMERICA...
THEN WITH THE CHARLESTON, WE'LL LINK TO THE TWENTIES, FOLLOWED BY A NUMBER ON TAP DANCING...
...NEXT, EXCERPTS FROM MUSICALS SUCH AS "SINGING IN THE RAIN" AND "WEST SIDE STORY," AND FINISH OFF WITH MODERN JAZZ FROM TODAY!
ANYONE HAVE ANY QUESTIONS?
YESSSSSSSSSS!
IS THOMAS YOUR BOYFRIEND?
I DON'T THINK THEY HEARD A THING YOU SAID, MARY!

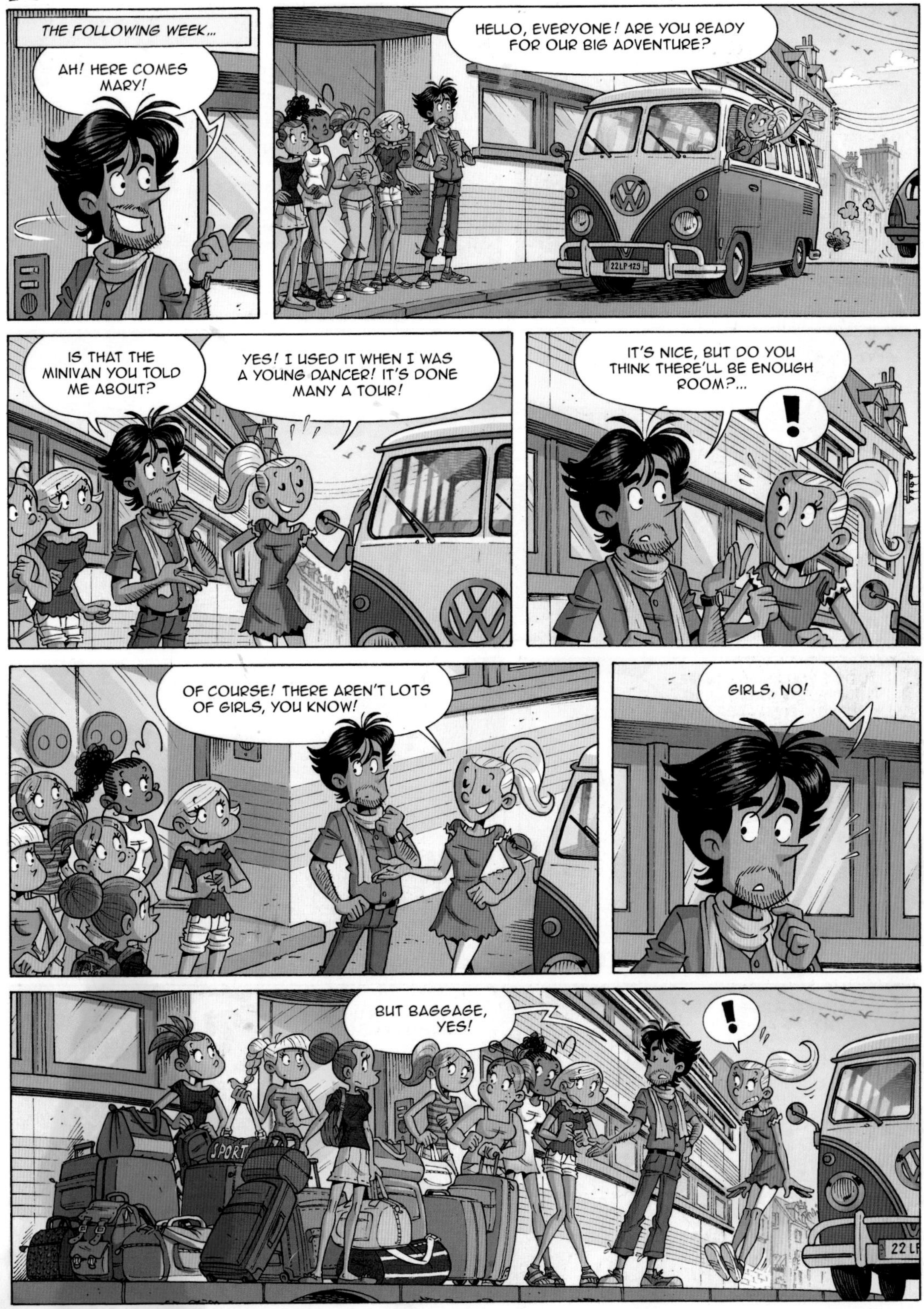

THE FOLLOWING WEEK...
AH! HERE COMES MARY!
HELLO, EVERYONE! ARE YOU READY FOR OUR BIG ADVENTURE?
22LP129
IS THAT THE MINIVAN YOU TOLD ME ABOUT?
YES! I USED IT WHEN I WAS A YOUNG DANCER! IT'S DONE MANY A TOUR!
IT'S NICE, BUT DO YOU THINK THERE'LL BE ENOUGH ROOM?...
!
OF COURSE! THERE AREN'T LOTS OF GIRLS, YOU KNOW!
GIRLS, NO!
BUT BAGGAGE, YES!
!
SPORT

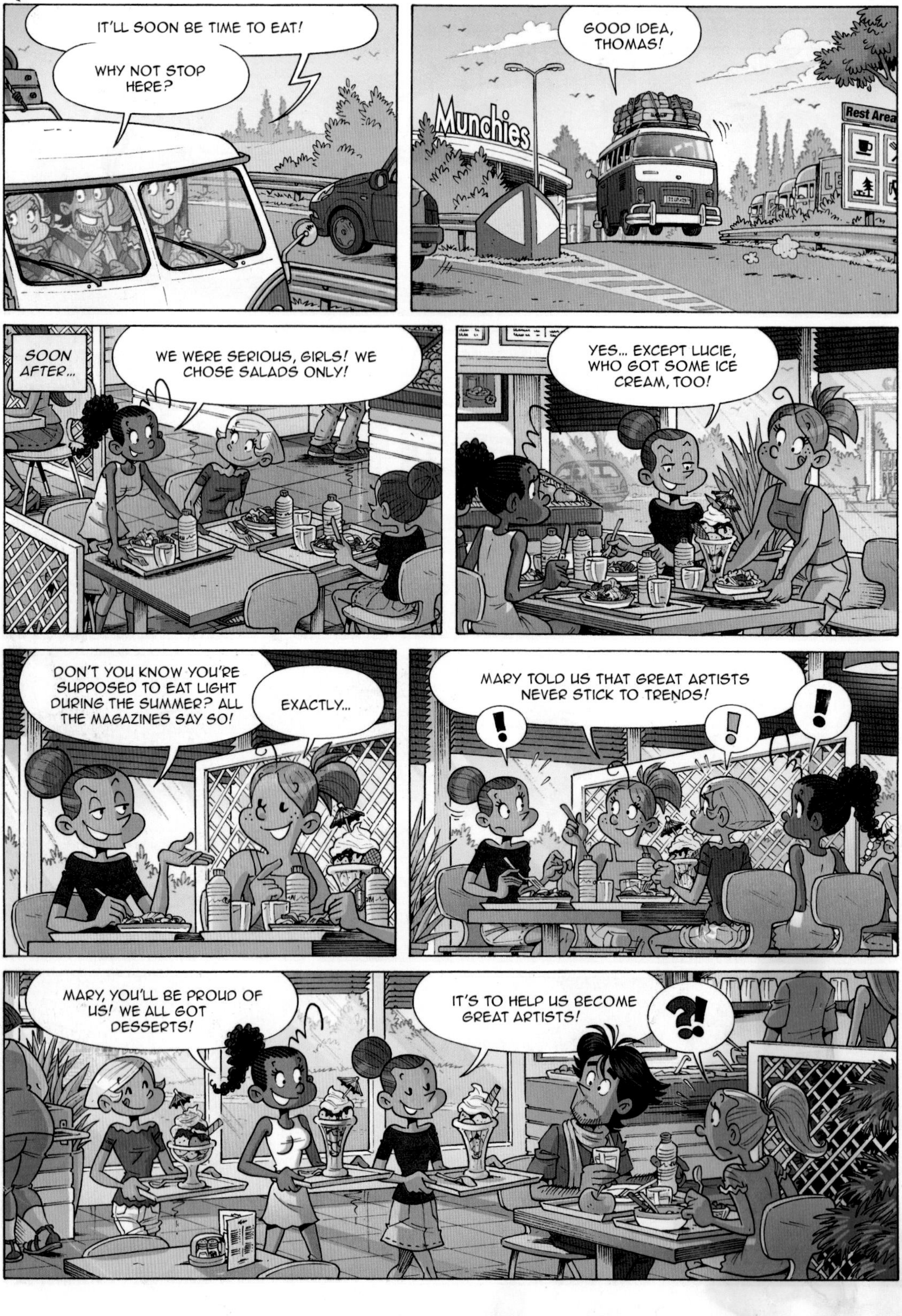
IT'LL SOON BE TIME TO EAT!
WHY NOT STOP HERE?
GOOD IDEA, THOMAS!
Munchies
Rest Area
SOON AFTER...
WE WERE SERIOUS, GIRLS! WE CHOSE SALADS ONLY!
YES... EXCEPT LUCIE, WHO GOT SOME ICE CREAM, TOO!
DON'T YOU KNOW YOU'RE SUPPOSED TO EAT LIGHT DURING THE SUMMER? ALL THE MAGAZINES SAY SO!
EXACTLY...
MARY TOLD US THAT GREAT ARTISTS NEVER STICK TO TRENDS!
!
!
!
MARY, YOU'LL BE PROUD OF US! WE ALL GOT DESSERTS!
IT'S TO HELP US BECOME GREAT ARTISTS!
?!

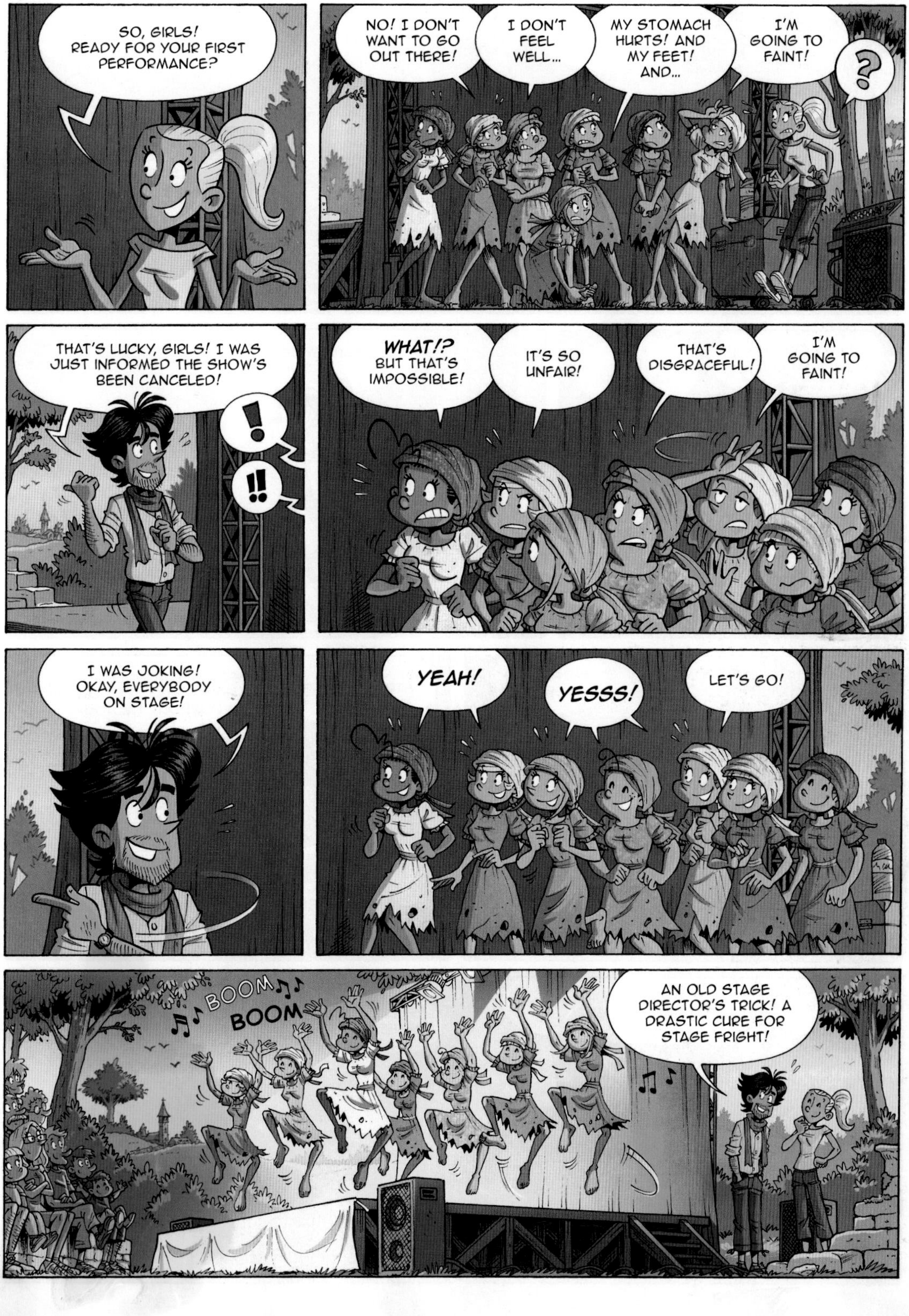
SO, GIRLS! READY FOR YOUR FIRST PERFORMANCE?
NO! I DON'T WANT TO GO OUT THERE!
I DON'T FEEL WELL...
MY STOMACH HURTS! AND MY FEET! AND...
I'M GOING TO FAINT!
?
THAT'S LUCKY, GIRLS! I WAS JUST INFORMED THE SHOW'S BEEN CANCELED!
!
!!
WHAT!? BUT THAT'S IMPOSSIBLE!
IT'S SO UNFAIR!
THAT'S DISGRACEFUL!
I'M GOING TO FAINT!
I WAS JOKING! OKAY, EVERYBODY ON STAGE!
YEAH!
YESSS!
LET'S GO!
BOOM
BOOM
AN OLD STAGE DIRECTOR'S TRICK! A DRASTIC CURE FOR STAGE FRIGHT!

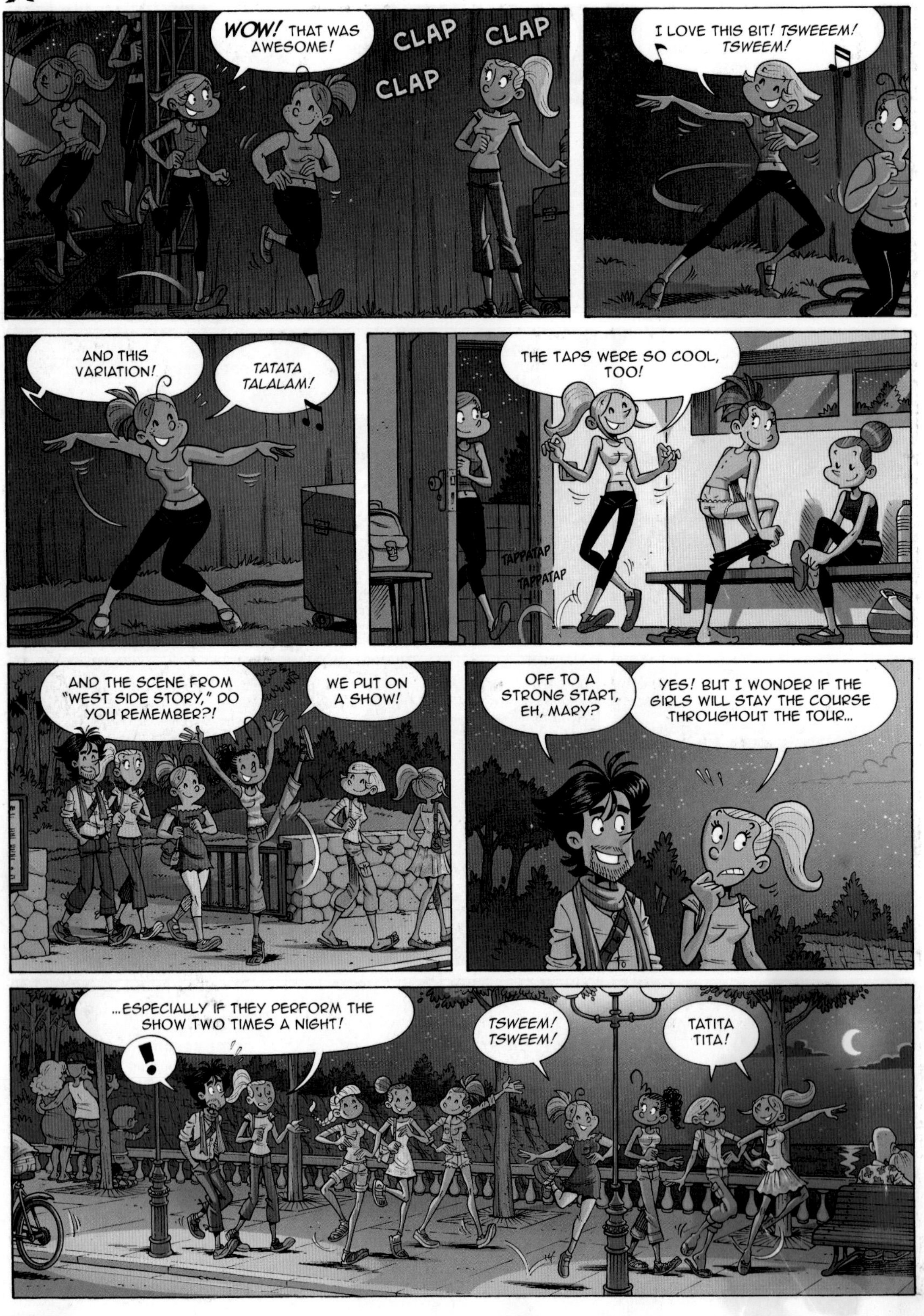
WOW! THAT WAS AWESOME!
CLAP CLAP
CLAP
I LOVE THIS BIT! TSWEEEM! TSWEEM!
AND THIS VARIATION!
TATATA TALALAM!
THE TAPS WERE SO COOL, TOO!
TAPPATAP !!! TAPPATAP
AND THE SCENE FROM "WEST SIDE STORY," DO YOU REMEMBER?!
WE PUT ON A SHOW!
OFF TO A STRONG START, EH, MARY?
YES! BUT I WONDER IF THE GIRLS WILL STAY THE COURSE THROUGHOUT THE TOUR...
...ESPECIALLY IF THEY PERFORM THE SHOW TWO TIMES A NIGHT!
!
TSWEEM! TSWEEM!
TATITA TITA!

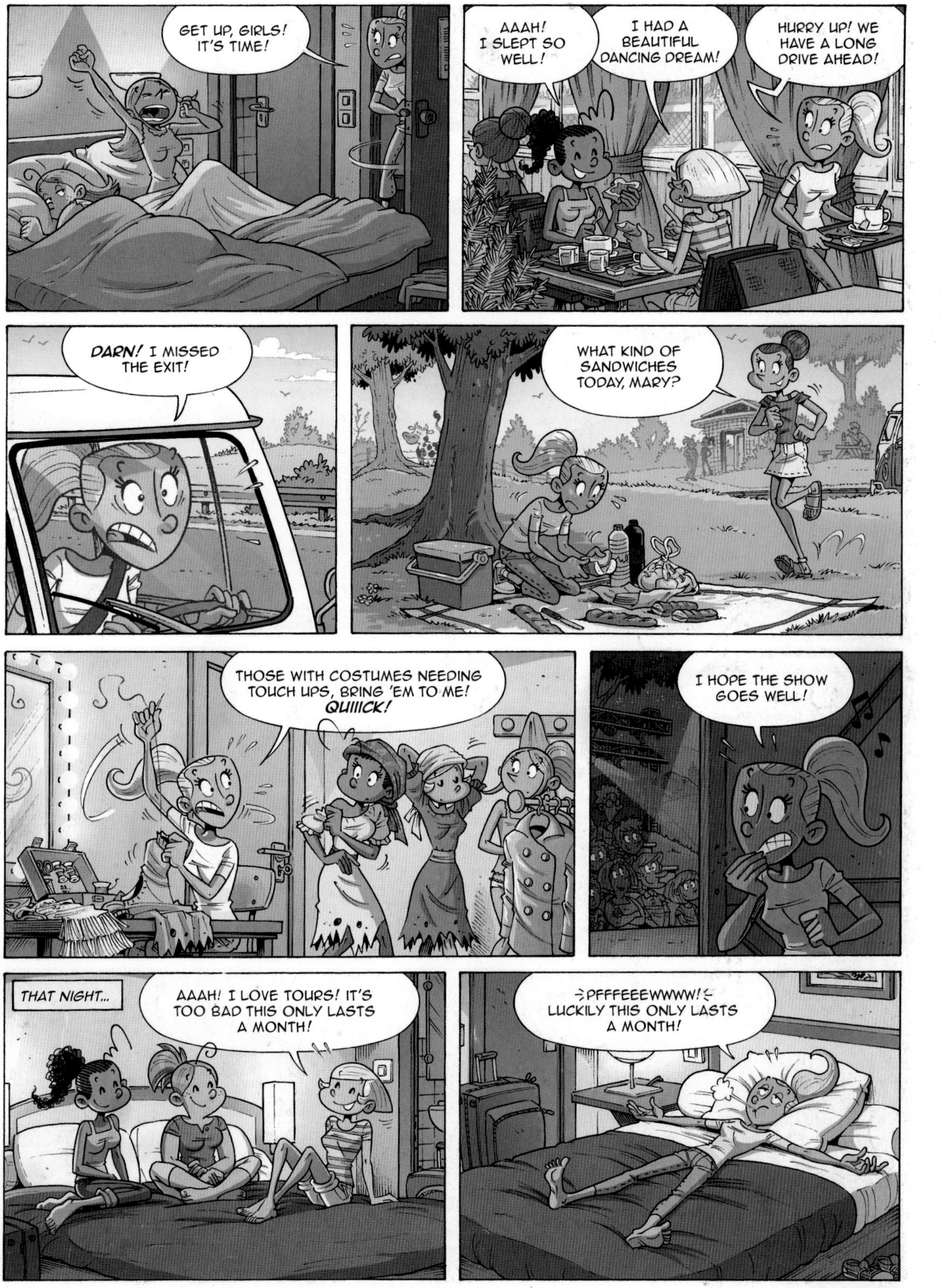
GET UP, GIRLS! IT'S TIME!
AAAH! I SLEPT SO WELL!
I HAD A BEAUTIFUL DANCING DREAM!
HURRY UP! WE HAVE A LONG DRIVE AHEAD!
DARN! I MISSED THE EXIT!
WHAT KIND OF SANDWICHES TODAY, MARY?
THOSE WITH COSTUMES NEEDING TOUCH UPS, BRING 'EM TO ME! QUIIICK!
I HOPE THE SHOW GOES WELL!
THAT NIGHT...
AAAH! I LOVE TOURS! IT'S TOO BAD THIS ONLY LASTS A MONTH!
PFFFEEEWWWW! LUCKILY THIS ONLY LASTS A MONTH!

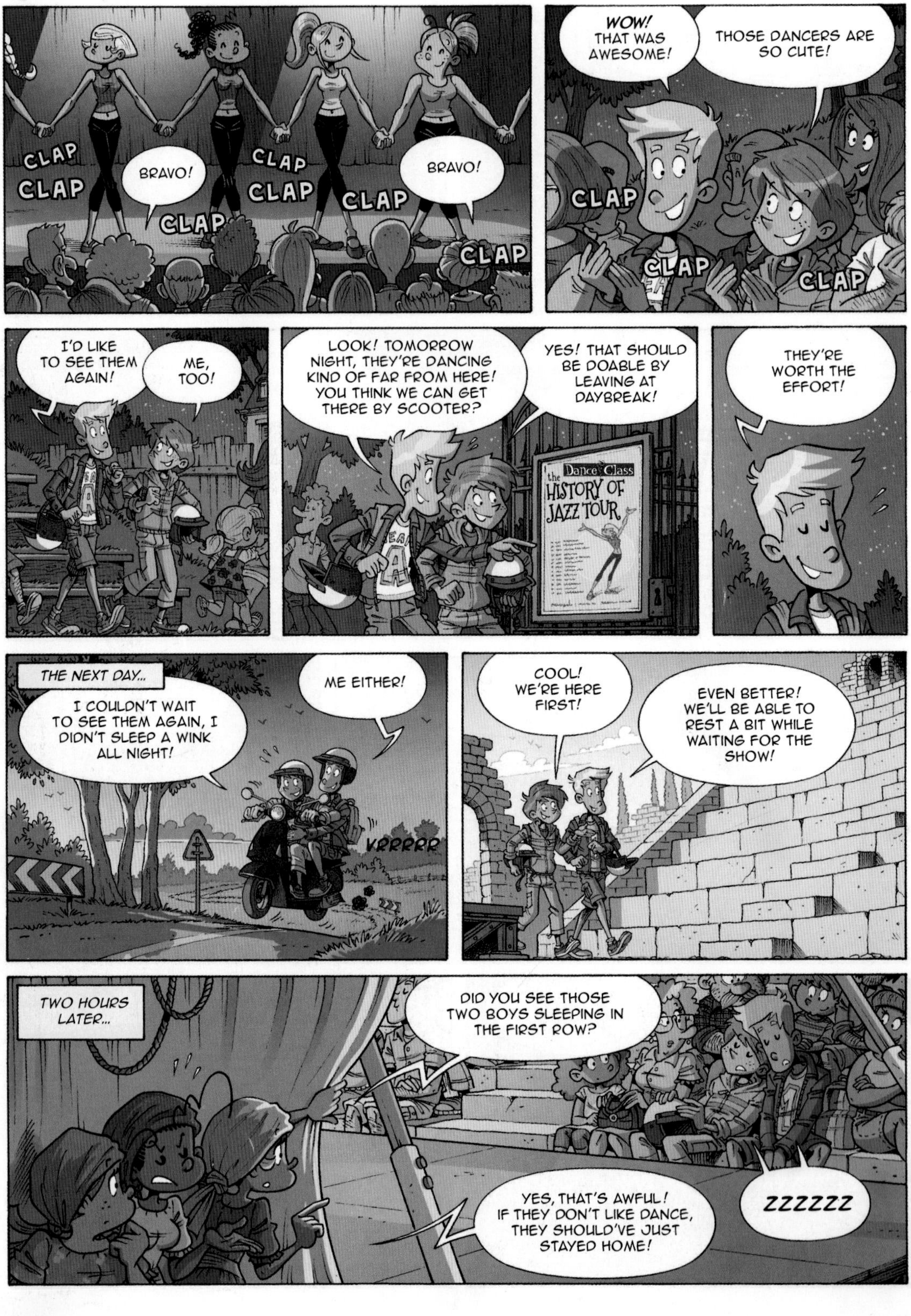
CLAP
CLAP
BRAVO!
CLAP
CLAP
CLAP
CLAP
BRAVO!
CLAP
CLAP
WOW! THAT WAS AWESOME!
THOSE DANCERS ARE SO CUTE!
CLAP
CLAP
CLAP
I'D LIKE TO SEE THEM AGAIN!
ME, TOO!
LOOK! TOMORROW NIGHT, THEY'RE DANCING KIND OF FAR FROM HERE! YOU THINK WE CAN GET THERE BY SCOOTER?
YES! THAT SHOULD BE DOABLE BY LEAVING AT DAYBREAK!
Dance Class
the HISTORY OF JAZZ TOUR
THEY'RE WORTH THE EFFORT!
THE NEXT DAY...
I COULDN'T WAIT TO SEE THEM AGAIN, I DIDN'T SLEEP A WINK ALL NIGHT!
ME EITHER!
VRRRRR
COOL! WE'RE HERE FIRST!
EVEN BETTER! WE'LL BE ABLE TO REST A BIT WHILE WAITING FOR THE SHOW!
TWO HOURS LATER...
DID YOU SEE THOSE TWO BOYS SLEEPING IN THE FIRST ROW?
YES, THAT'S AWFUL! IF THEY DON'T LIKE DANCE, THEY SHOULD'VE JUST STAYED HOME!
ZZZZZZ

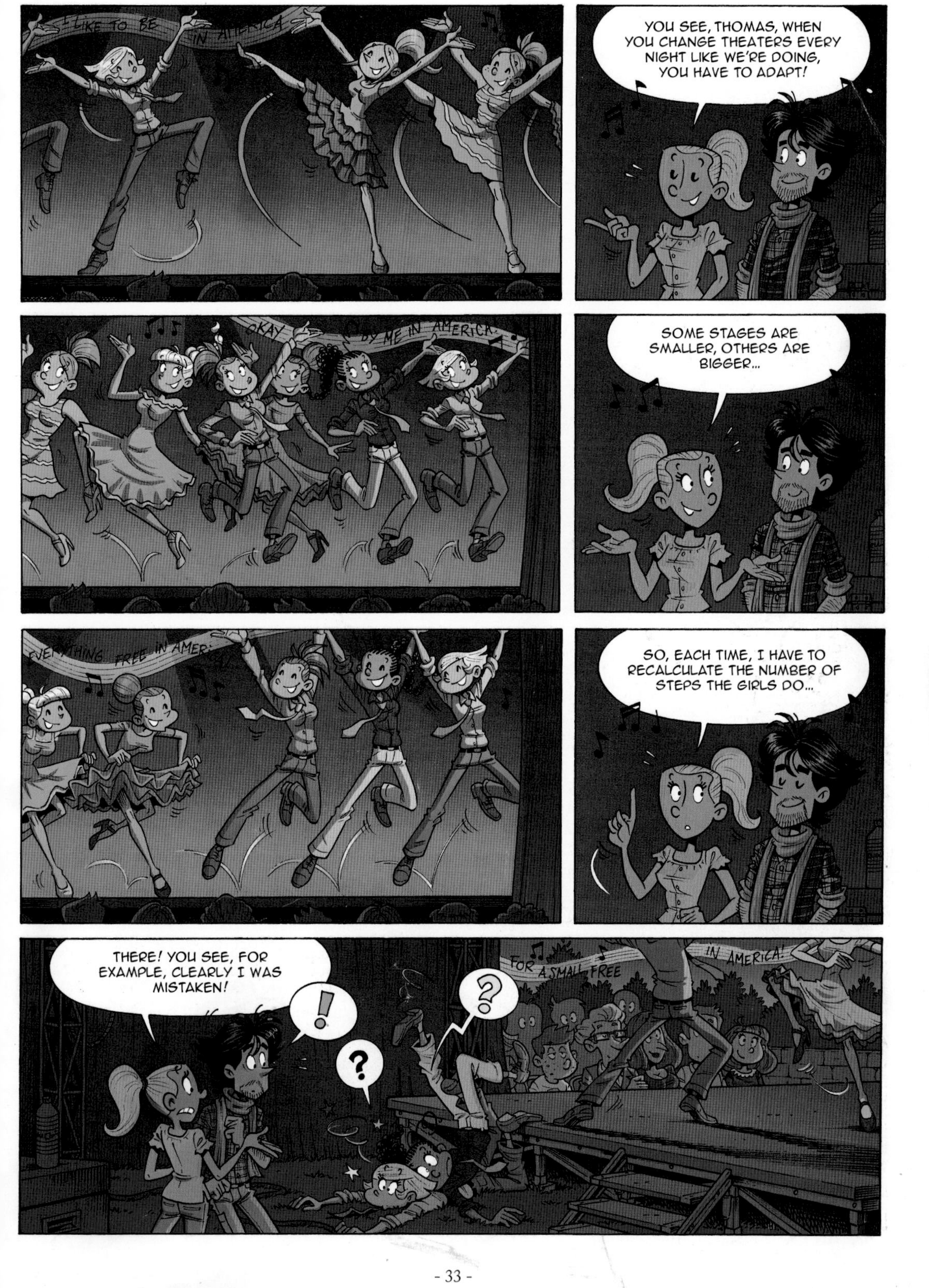
I LIKE TO BE IN AMERICA
YOU SEE, THOMAS, WHEN YOU CHANGE THEATERS EVERY NIGHT LIKE WE'RE DOING, YOU HAVE TO ADAPT!
OKAY BY ME IN AMERICA
SOME STAGES ARE SMALLER, OTHERS ARE BIGGER...
SO, EACH TIME, I HAVE TO RECALCULATE THE NUMBER OF STEPS THE GIRLS DO...
THERE! YOU SEE, FOR EXAMPLE, CLEARLY I WAS MISTAKEN!
!
?
?
FOR A SMALL FREE
IN AMERICA!

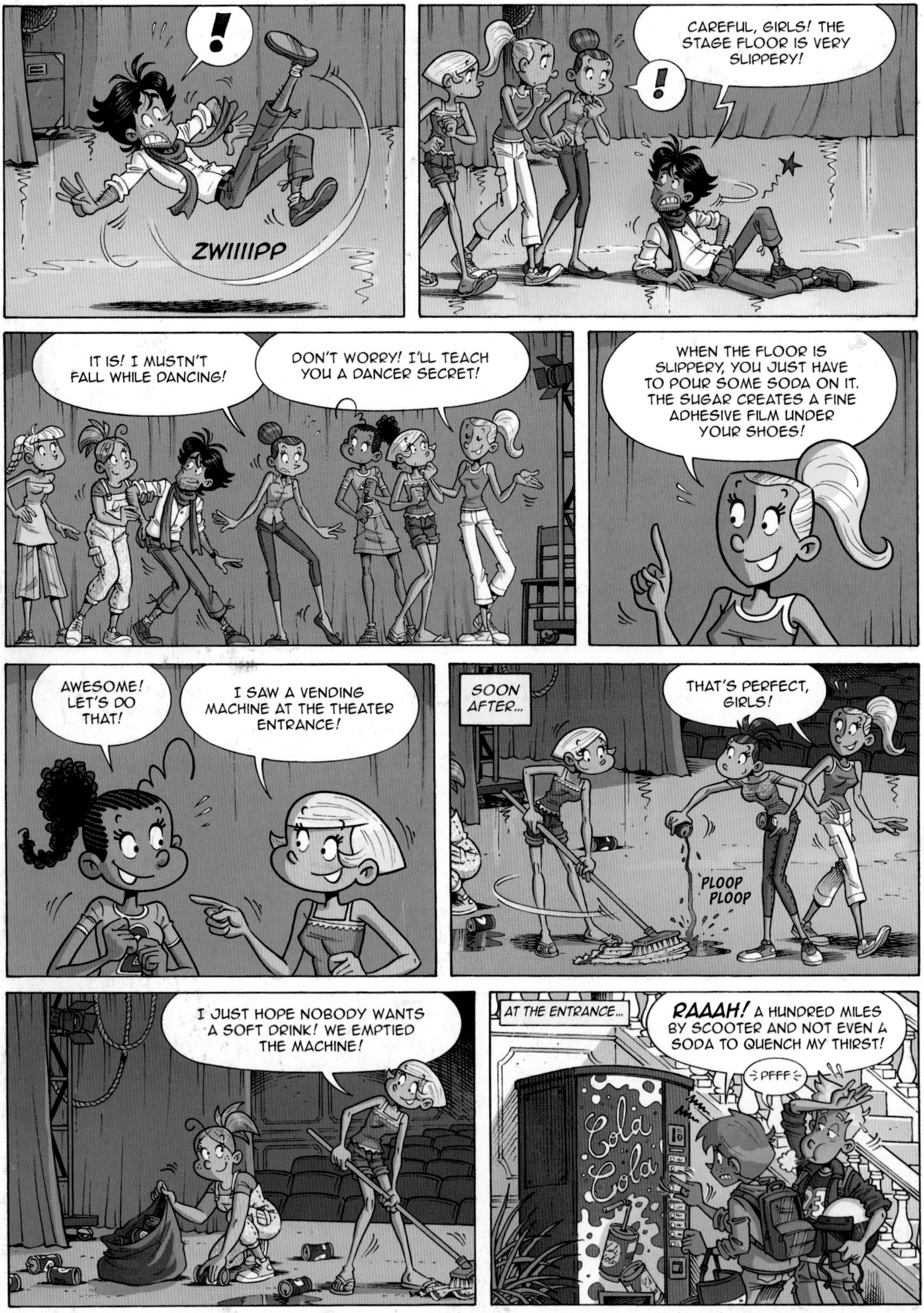
!
ZWIIIIPP
CAREFUL, GIRLS! THE STAGE FLOOR IS VERY SLIPPERY!
!
IT IS! I MUSTN'T FALL WHILE DANCING!
DON'T WORRY! I'LL TEACH YOU A DANCER SECRET!
WHEN THE FLOOR IS SLIPPERY, YOU JUST HAVE TO POUR SOME SODA ON IT. THE SUGAR CREATES A FINE ADHESIVE FILM UNDER YOUR SHOES!
AWESOME! LET'S DO THAT!
I SAW A VENDING MACHINE AT THE THEATER ENTRANCE!
SOON AFTER...
THAT'S PERFECT, GIRLS!
PLOOP PLOOP
I JUST HOPE NOBODY WANTS A SOFT DRINK! WE EMPTIED THE MACHINE!
AT THE ENTRANCE...
RAAAH! A HUNDRED MILES BY SCOOTER AND NOT EVEN A SODA TO QUENCH MY THIRST!
PFFF
Cola Cola

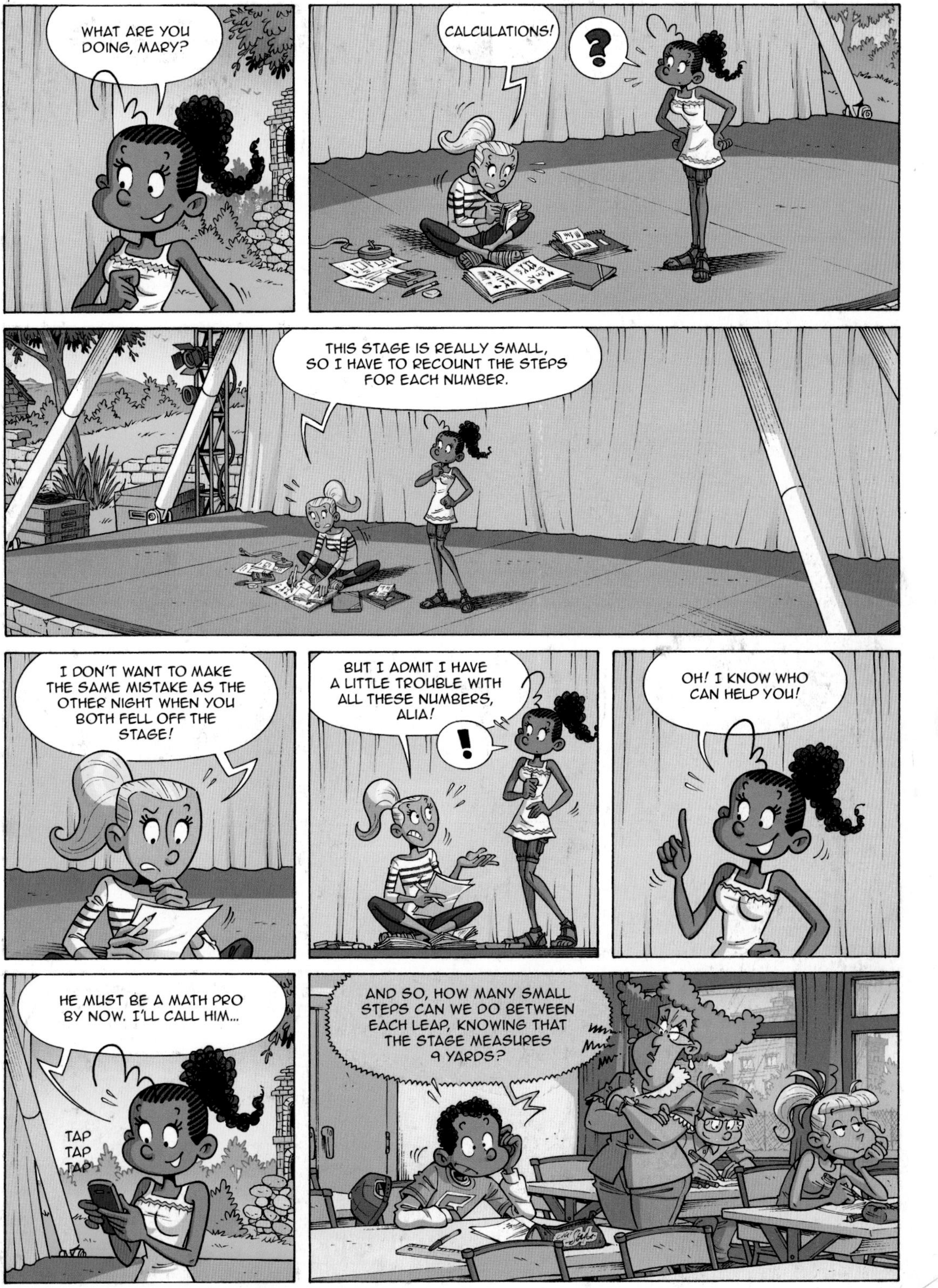
WHAT ARE YOU DOING, MARY?
CALCULATIONS!
?
THIS STAGE IS REALLY SMALL, SO I HAVE TO RECOUNT THE STEPS FOR EACH NUMBER.
I DON'T WANT TO MAKE THE SAME MISTAKE AS THE OTHER NIGHT WHEN YOU BOTH FELL OFF THE STAGE!
BUT I ADMIT I HAVE A LITTLE TROUBLE WITH ALL THESE NUMBERS, ALIA!
!
OH! I KNOW WHO CAN HELP YOU!
HE MUST BE A MATH PRO BY NOW. I'LL CALL HIM...
TAP
TAP
TAP
AND SO, HOW MANY SMALL STEPS CAN WE DO BETWEEN EACH LEAP, KNOWING THAT THE STAGE MEASURES 9 YARDS?

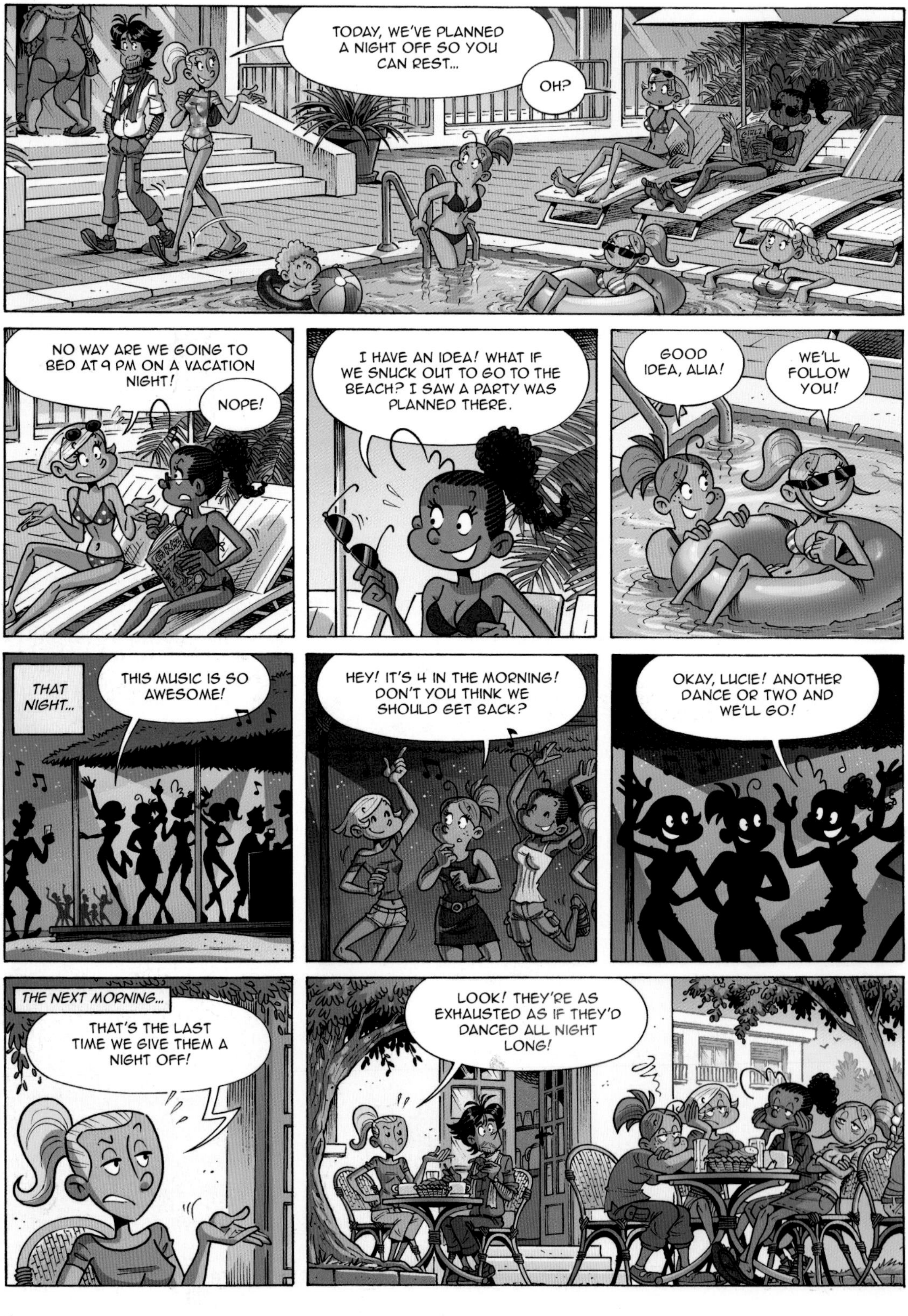
TODAY, WE'VE PLANNED A NIGHT OFF SO YOU CAN REST...
OH?
NO WAY ARE WE GOING TO BED AT 9 PM ON A VACATION NIGHT!
NOPE!
I HAVE AN IDEA! WHAT IF WE SNUCK OUT TO GO TO THE BEACH? I SAW A PARTY WAS PLANNED THERE.
GOOD IDEA, ALIA!
WE'LL FOLLOW YOU!
THAT NIGHT...
THIS MUSIC IS SO AWESOME!
HEY! IT'S 4 IN THE MORNING! DON'T YOU THINK WE SHOULD GET BACK?
OKAY, LUCIE! ANOTHER DANCE OR TWO AND WE'LL GO!
THE NEXT MORNING...
THAT'S THE LAST TIME WE GIVE THEM A NIGHT OFF!
LOOK! THEY'RE AS EXHAUSTED AS IF THEY'D DANCED ALL NIGHT LONG!

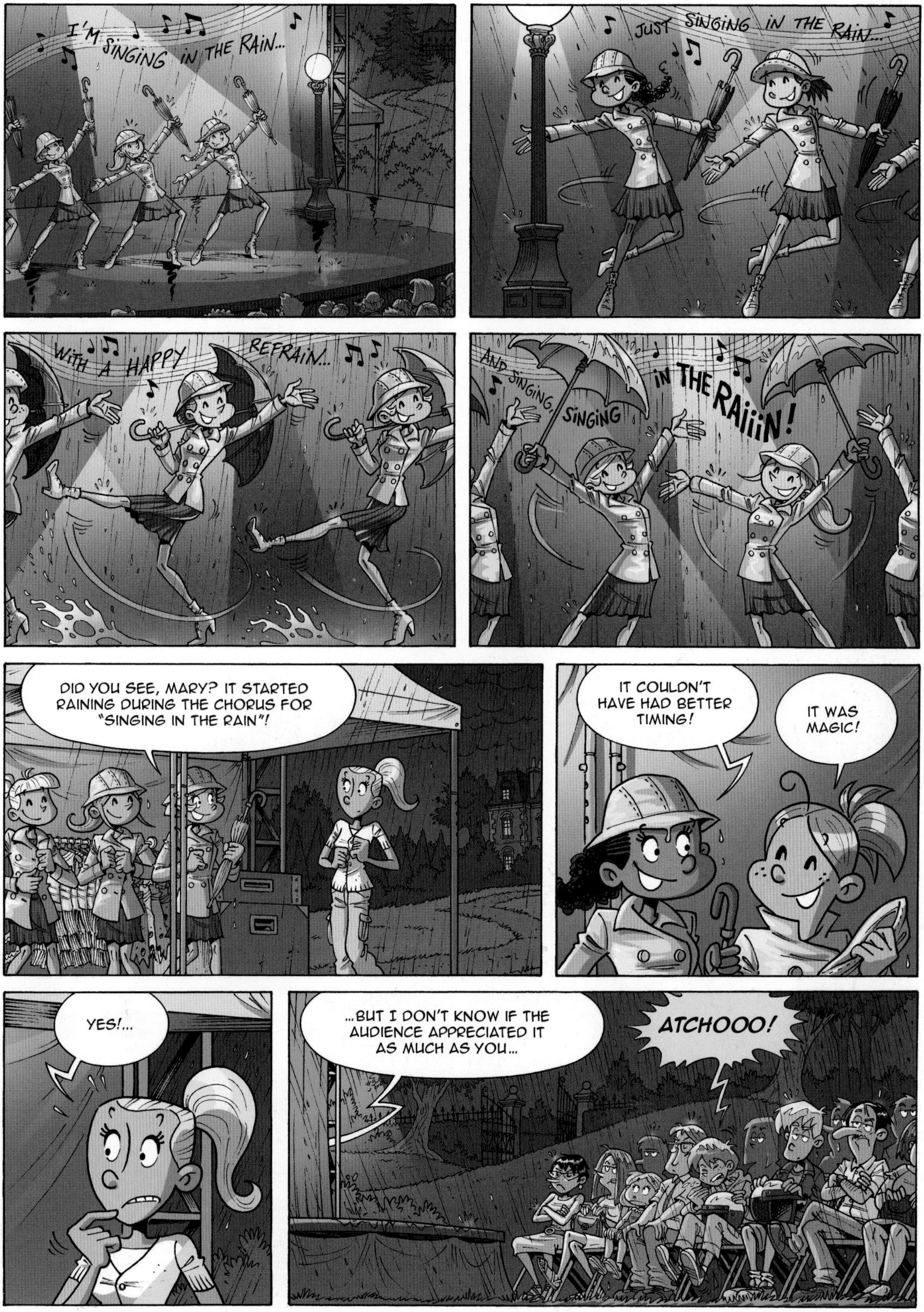
I'M SINGING IN THE RAIN...
JUST SINGING IN THE RAIN...
WITH A HAPPY REFRAIN...
AND SINGING, SINGING IN THE RAIIIN!
DID YOU SEE, MARY? IT STARTED RAINING DURING THE CHORUS FOR "SINGING IN THE RAIN"!
IT COULDN'T HAVE HAD BETTER TIMING!
IT WAS MAGIC!
YES!...
...BUT I DON'T KNOW IF THE AUDIENCE APPRECIATED IT AS MUCH AS YOU...
ATCHOOO!

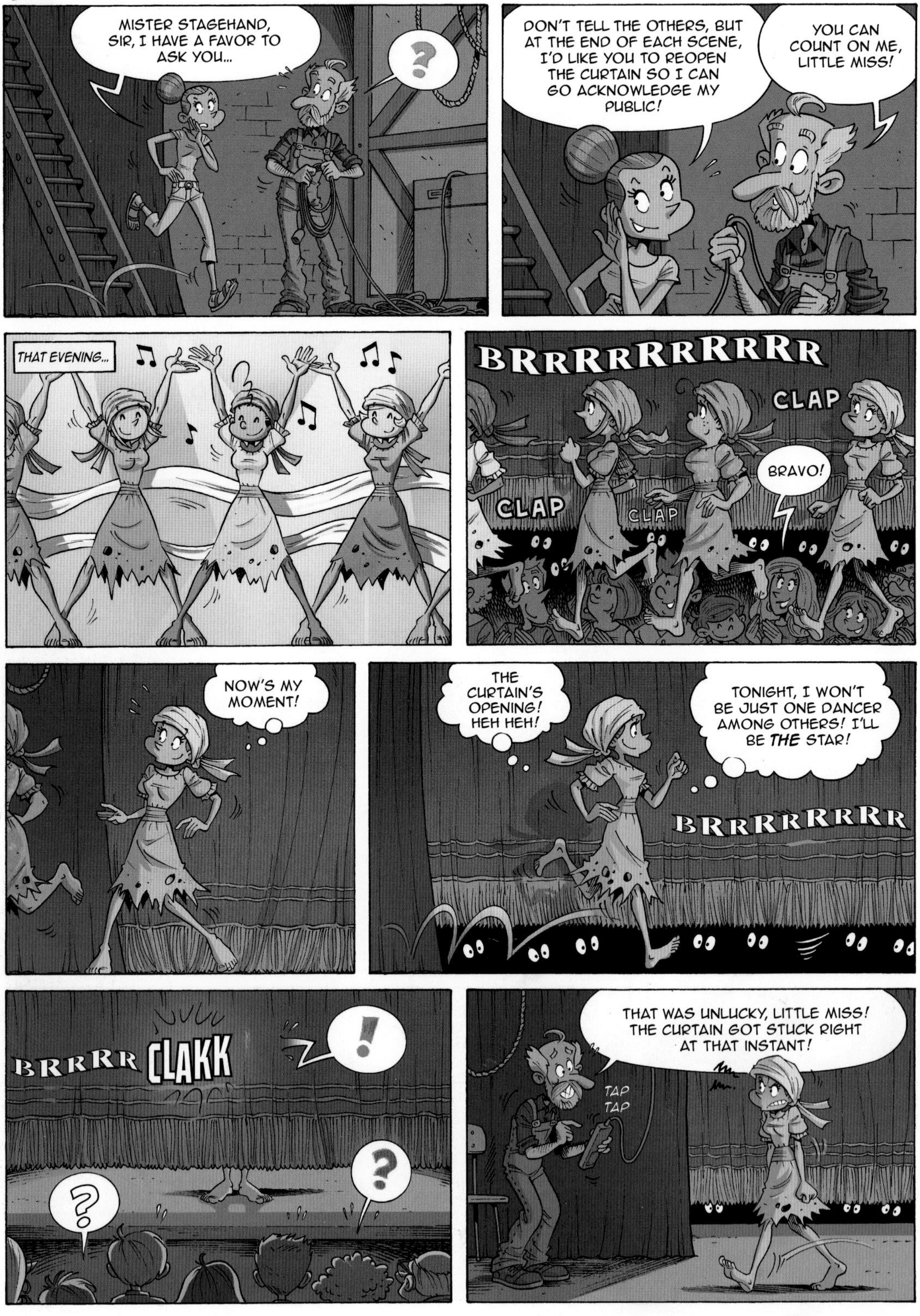
MISTER STAGEHAND, SIR, I HAVE A FAVOR TO ASK YOU...
?
DON'T TELL THE OTHERS, BUT AT THE END OF EACH SCENE, I'D LIKE YOU TO REOPEN THE CURTAIN SO I CAN GO ACKNOWLEDGE MY PUBLIC!
YOU CAN COUNT ON ME, LITTLE MISS!
THAT EVENING...
BRRRRRRRRRRR
CLAP
BRAVO!
CLAP
CLAP
NOW'S MY MOMENT!
THE CURTAIN'S OPENING! HEH HEH!
TONIGHT, I WON'T BE JUST ONE DANCER AMONG OTHERS! I'LL BE THE STAR!
BRRRRRRRRR
BRRRRR CLAKK
!
?
?
THAT WAS UNLUCKY, LITTLE MISS! THE CURTAIN GOT STUCK RIGHT AT THAT INSTANT!
TAP TAP

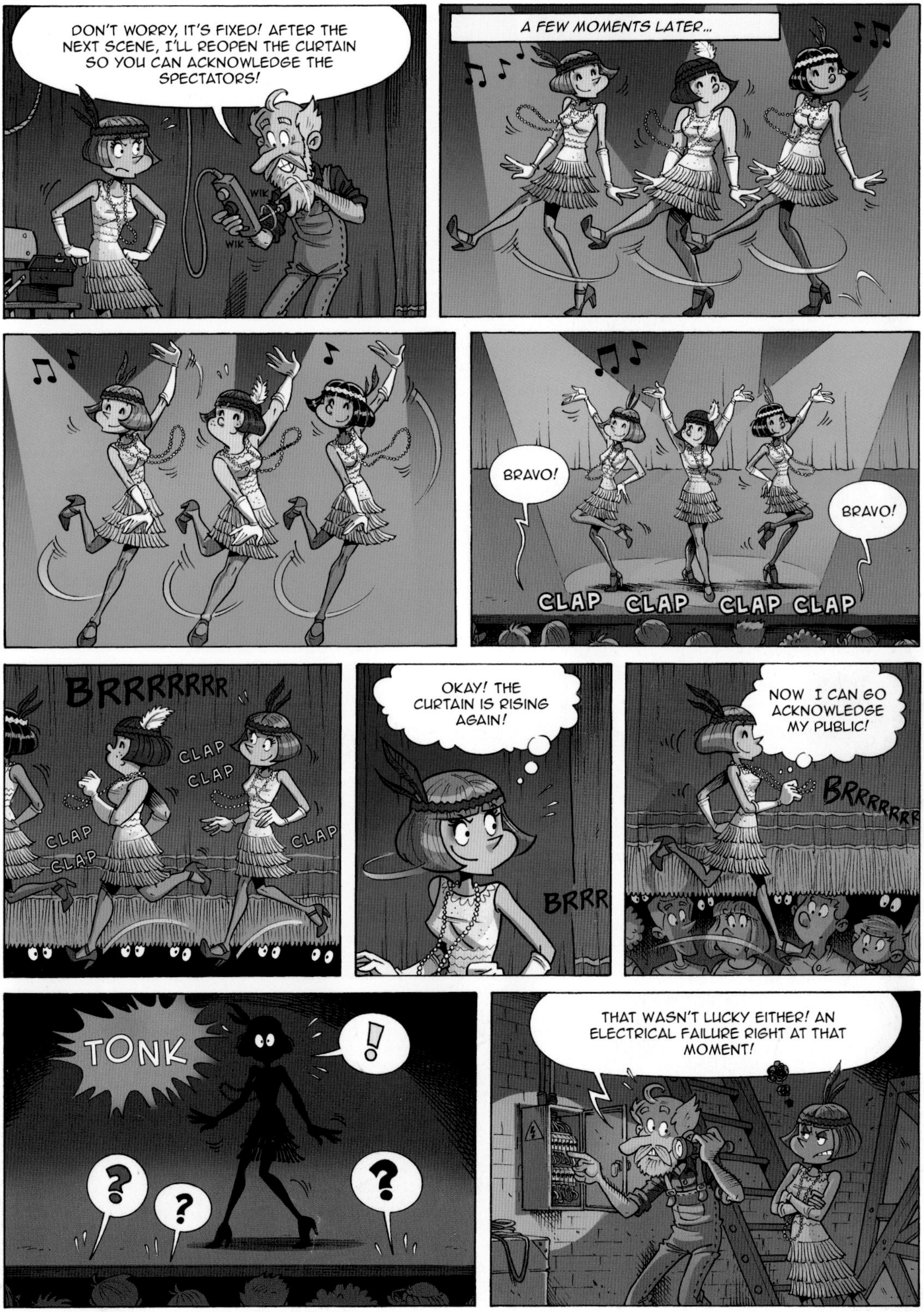
DON'T WORRY, IT'S FIXED! AFTER THE NEXT SCENE, I'LL REOPEN THE CURTAIN SO YOU CAN ACKNOWLEDGE THE SPECTATORS!
WIK
WIK
A FEW MOMENTS LATER...
BRAVO!
BRAVO!
CLAP CLAP CLAP CLAP
BRRRRRRR
CLAP
CLAP
CLAP
CLAP
CLAP
OKAY! THE CURTAIN IS RISING AGAIN!
BRRR
NOW I CAN GO ACKNOWLEDGE MY PUBLIC!
BRRRRRRR
TONK
!
?
?
?
THAT WASN'T LUCKY EITHER! AN ELECTRICAL FAILURE RIGHT AT THAT MOMENT!

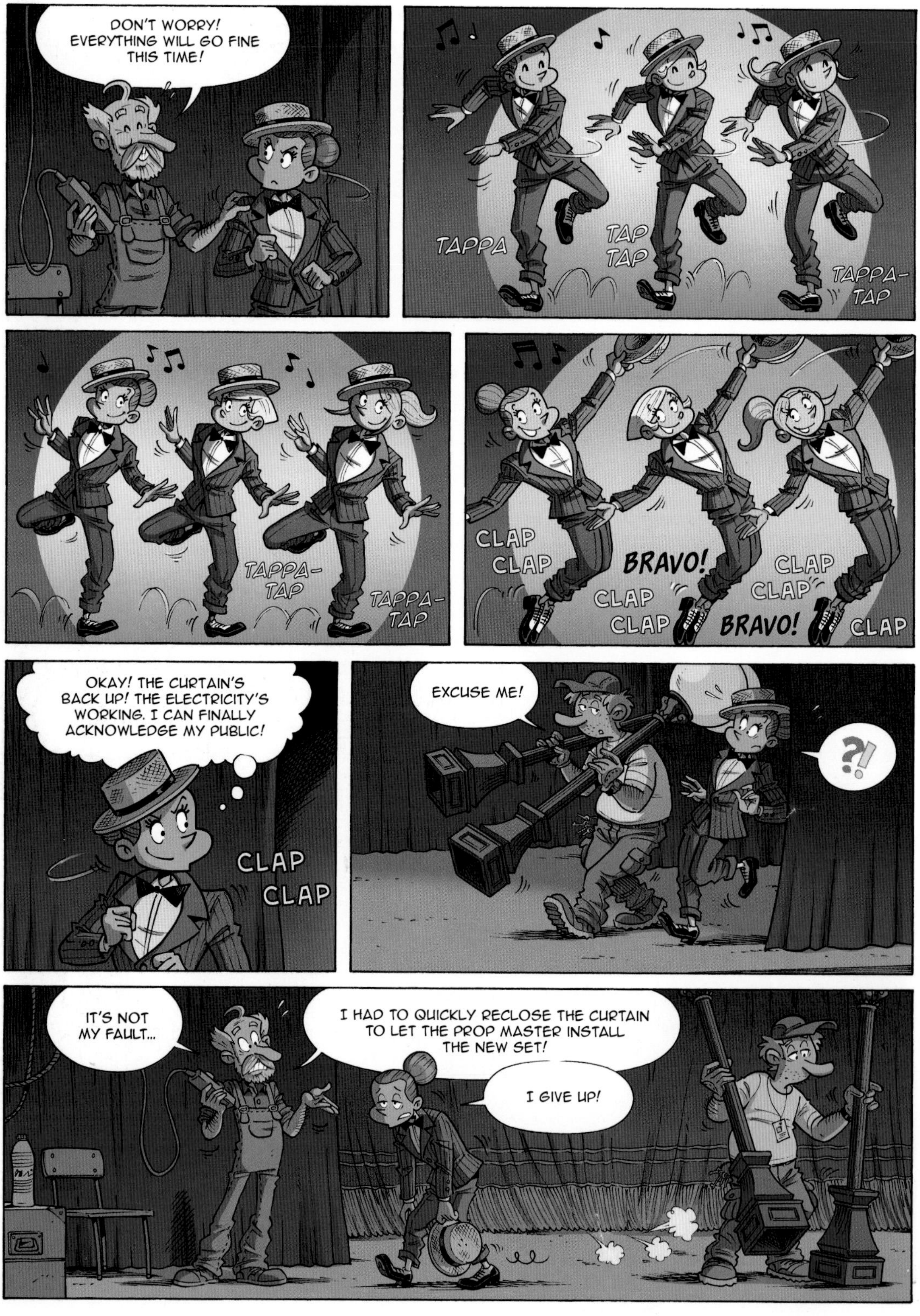
DON'T WORRY! EVERYTHING WILL GO FINE THIS TIME!
TAPPA
TAP TAP
TAPPA-TAP
TAPPA-TAP
TAPPA-TAP
CLAP CLAP
BRAVO!
CLAP CLAP
CLAP CLAP
BRAVO!
CLAP
OKAY! THE CURTAIN'S BACK UP! THE ELECTRICITY'S WORKING. I CAN FINALLY ACKNOWLEDGE MY PUBLIC!
CLAP CLAP
EXCUSE ME!
?!
IT'S NOT MY FAULT...
I HAD TO QUICKLY RECLOSE THE CURTAIN TO LET THE PROP MASTER INSTALL THE NEW SET!
I GIVE UP!

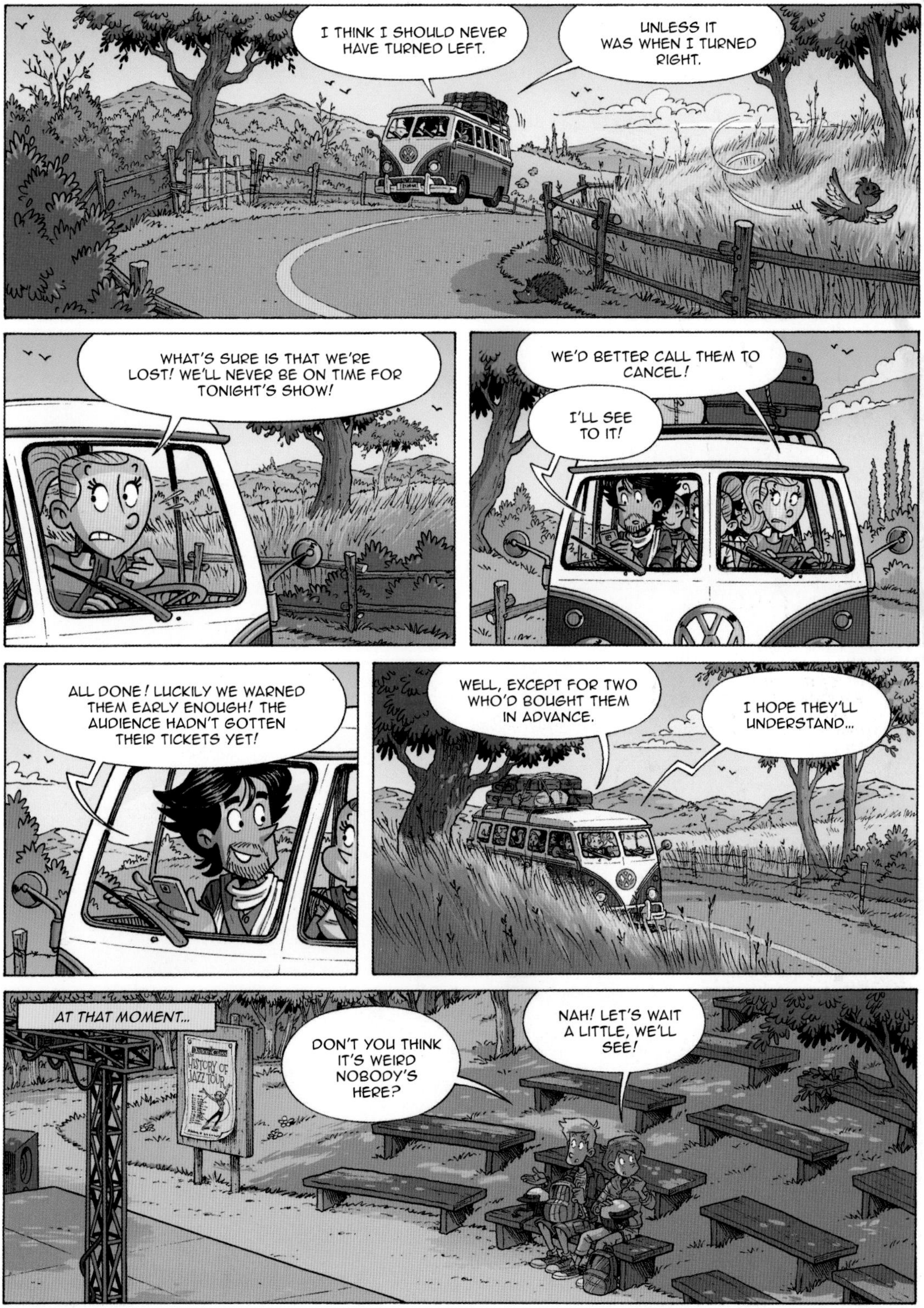
I THINK I SHOULD NEVER HAVE TURNED LEFT.
UNLESS IT WAS WHEN I TURNED RIGHT.
WHAT'S SURE IS THAT WE'RE LOST! WE'LL NEVER BE ON TIME FOR TONIGHT'S SHOW!
WE'D BETTER CALL THEM TO CANCEL!
I'LL SEE TO IT!
ALL DONE! LUCKILY WE WARNED THEM EARLY ENOUGH! THE AUDIENCE HADN'T GOTTEN THEIR TICKETS YET!
WELL, EXCEPT FOR TWO WHO'D BOUGHT THEM IN ADVANCE.
I HOPE THEY'LL UNDERSTAND...
AT THAT MOMENT...
HISTORY OF JAZZ TOUR
DON'T YOU THINK IT'S WEIRD NOBODY'S HERE?
NAH! LET'S WAIT A LITTLE, WE'LL SEE!

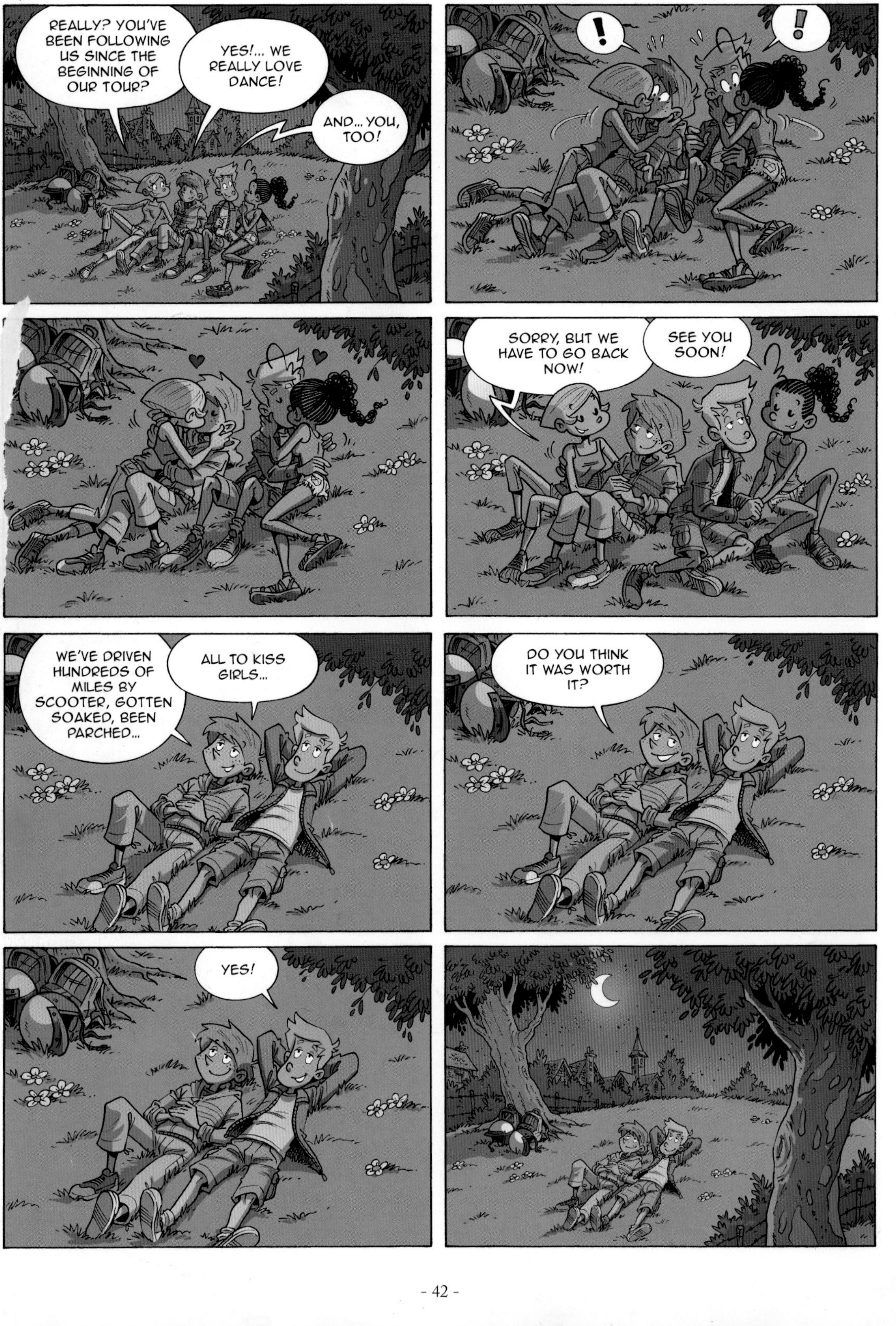
REALLY? YOU'VE BEEN FOLLOWING US SINCE THE BEGINNING OF OUR TOUR?
YES!... WE REALLY LOVE DANCE!
AND... YOU, TOO!
!
!
SORRY, BUT WE HAVE TO GO BACK NOW!
SEE YOU SOON!
WE'VE DRIVEN HUNDREDS OF MILES BY SCOOTER, GOTTEN SOAKED, BEEN PARCHED...
ALL TO KISS GIRLS...
DO YOU THINK IT WAS WORTH IT?
YES!

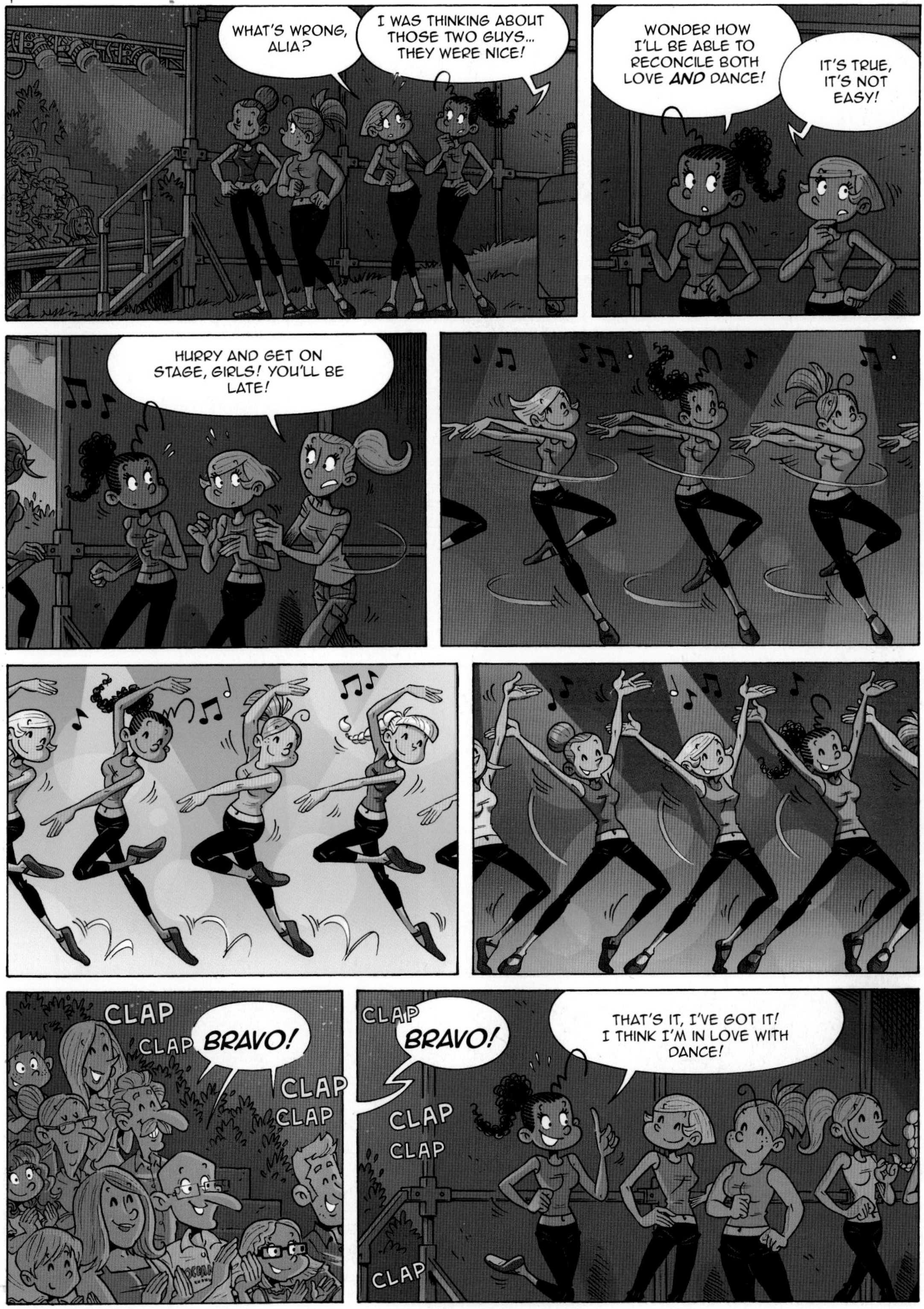

WHAT'S WRONG, ALIA?
I WAS THINKING ABOUT THOSE TWO GUYS... THEY WERE NICE!
WONDER HOW I'LL BE ABLE TO RECONCILE BOTH LOVE ***AND*** DANCE!
IT'S TRUE, IT'S NOT EASY!
HURRY AND GET ON STAGE, GIRLS! YOU'LL BE LATE!
CLAP
CLAP
BRAVO!
CLAP
CLAP
CLAP
BRAVO!
CLAP
CLAP
THAT'S IT, I'VE GOT IT! I THINK I'M IN LOVE WITH DANCE!
CLAP

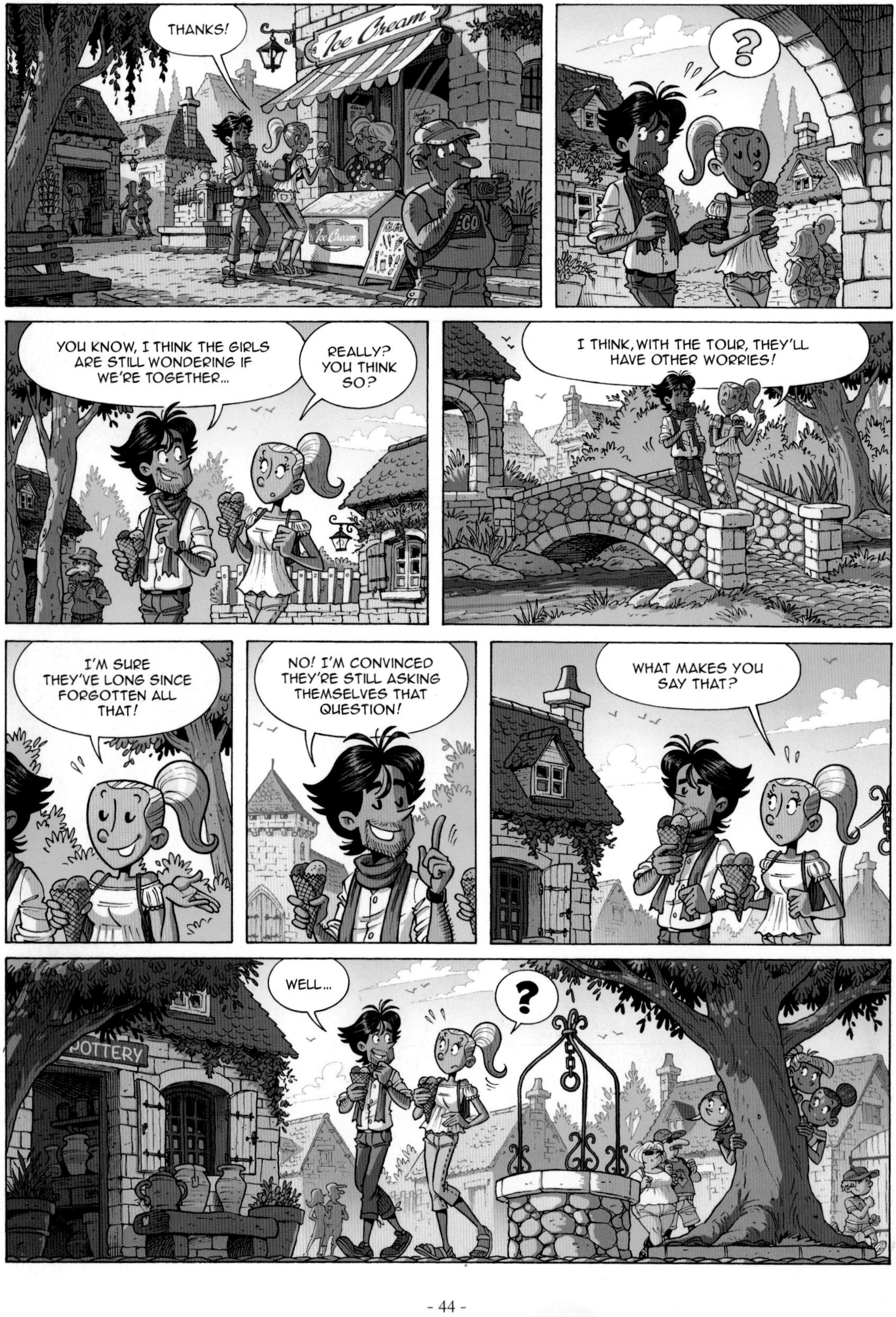
THANKS!
Ice Cream
Ice Cream
?
YOU KNOW, I THINK THE GIRLS ARE STILL WONDERING IF WE'RE TOGETHER...
REALLY? YOU THINK SO?
I THINK, WITH THE TOUR, THEY'LL HAVE OTHER WORRIES!
I'M SURE THEY'VE LONG SINCE FORGOTTEN ALL THAT!
NO! I'M CONVINCED THEY'RE STILL ASKING THEMSELVES THAT QUESTION!
WHAT MAKES YOU SAY THAT?
WELL...
?
POTTERY

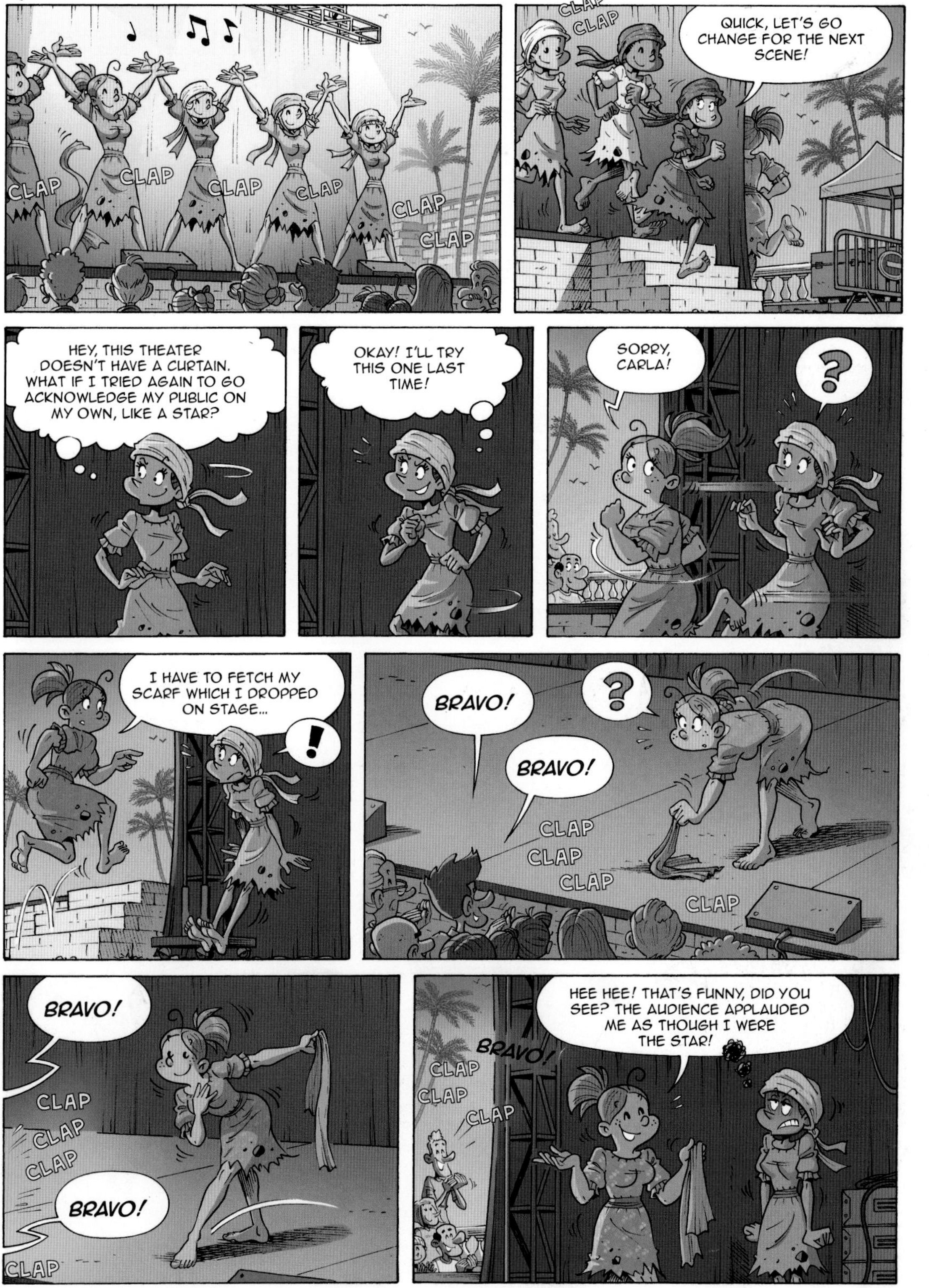
CLAP
CLAP
CLAP
CLAP
CLAP
CLAP
CLAP
CLAP
QUICK, LET'S GO CHANGE FOR THE NEXT SCENE!
HEY, THIS THEATER DOESN'T HAVE A CURTAIN. WHAT IF I TRIED AGAIN TO GO ACKNOWLEDGE MY PUBLIC ON MY OWN, LIKE A STAR?
OKAY! I'LL TRY THIS ONE LAST TIME!
SORRY, CARLA!
?
I HAVE TO FETCH MY SCARF WHICH I DROPPED ON STAGE...
!
BRAVO!
?
BRAVO!
CLAP
CLAP
CLAP
CLAP
BRAVO!
CLAP
CLAP
CLAP
BRAVO!
CLAP
HEE HEE! THAT'S FUNNY, DID YOU SEE? THE AUDIENCE APPLAUDED ME AS THOUGH I WERE THE STAR!
BRAVO!
CLAP
CLAP
CLAP

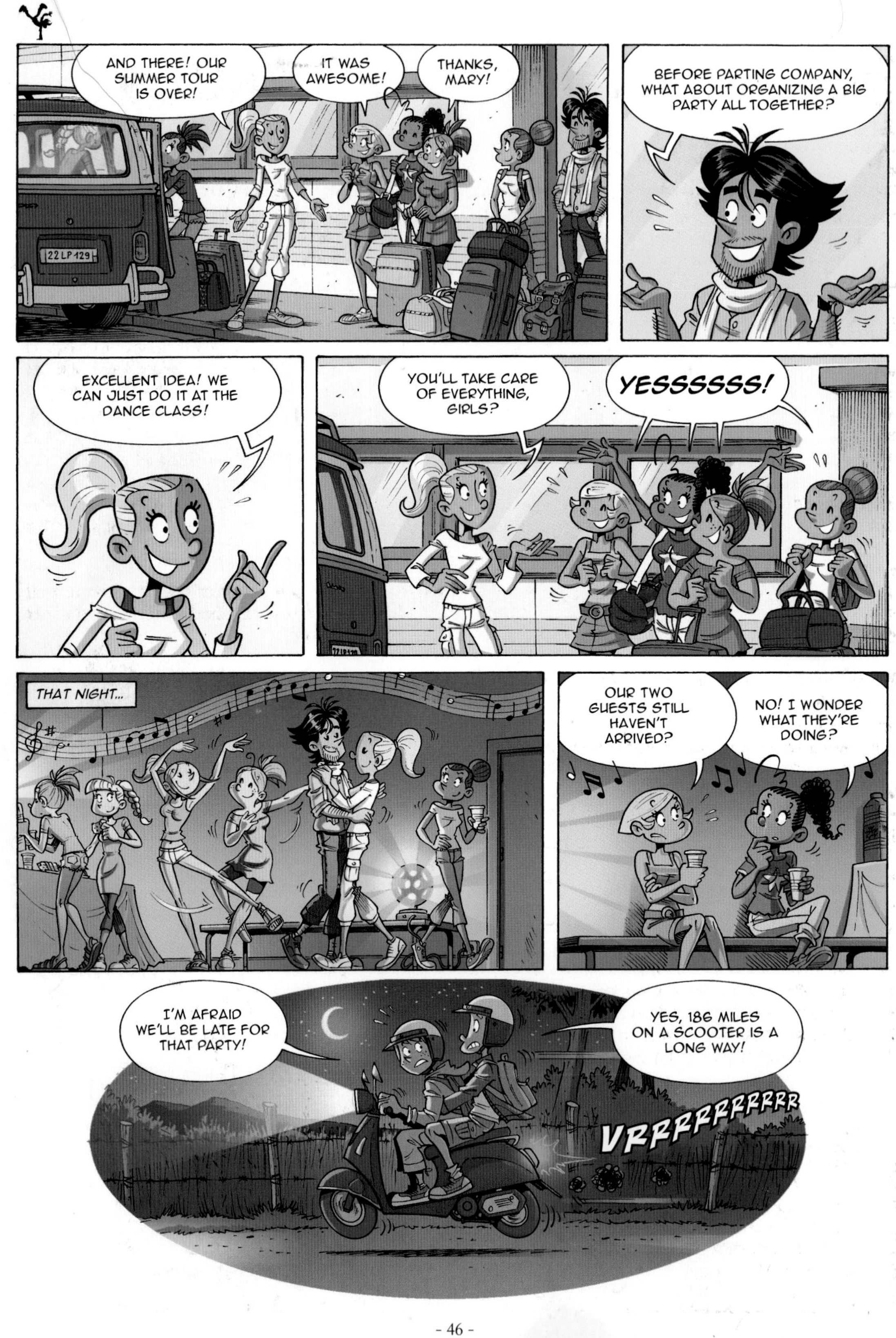
AND THERE! OUR SUMMER TOUR IS OVER!
IT WAS AWESOME!
THANKS, MARY!
BEFORE PARTING COMPANY, WHAT ABOUT ORGANIZING A BIG PARTY ALL TOGETHER?
EXCELLENT IDEA! WE CAN JUST DO IT AT THE DANCE CLASS!
YOU'LL TAKE CARE OF EVERYTHING, GIRLS?
YESSSSSS!
THAT NIGHT...
OUR TWO GUESTS STILL HAVEN'T ARRIVED?
NO! I WONDER WHAT THEY'RE DOING?
I'M AFRAID WE'LL BE LATE FOR THAT PARTY!
YES, 186 MILES ON A SCOOTER IS A LONG WAY!
VRRRRRRRRRR

WATCH OUT FOR PAPERCUTZ™

Welcome to the nimble and notably noble ninth DANCE CLASS graphic novel by Crip & Béka, and Maëla Cosson, from Papercutz, that talented troupe dedicated to publishing great graphic novels for all ages. I'm Jim Salicrup, the Editor-in-Chief of Papercutz and sometime soggy dance student… not from the rain—from perspiration! Dancing isn't as easy as it looks!

Speaking of which, I strongly advise against dancing in the rain, even if our friend Rebecca, co-star of the critically-acclaimed Papercutz graphic novel series ERNEST & REBECCA, also loves to prance about in wet weather. You'd think she'd learn by now, considering that her best friend Ernest is actually a germ, that such behavior could lead to ill health.

But sometimes humans are far from logical. Take Julie, Alia, Lucie, and the rest of the DANCE CLASS students. After a rigorous day of dance rehearsals, when the girls are given the night off, what do they decide to do…? That's right… they dance! Why? Because they love it! Dancing is a passion for these girls and there's almost nothing they'd rather be doing.

I can certainly relate. As passionate as Julie, Alia, and Lucie are about dancing, I'm equally crazed about comics and graphic novels! For example, every Wednesday after spending the morning editing Papercutz graphic novels, where do you think I go during my lunch break? If you guessed the comicbook store, you're absolutely right! (I do pick up lunch too. I'm not that crazy!)

I'm sure I've mentioned this before, but I can't help mentioning it again. Over the years I've been lucky enough to take Ballroom dance classes myself, and it wasn't until many years later that I realized why it seemed to provide a wonderful sense of balance to my life. Comics, even DANCE CLASS, is an art form where there's no sound or movement, while dance, is all about moving to sound. By having both in your life, you've got the best of both worlds.

For those of you wondering exactly who Ernest & Rebecca are (those guys I mentioned a few paragraphs ago), let's just say it's complicated. The best way to really get to know them is to find their graphic novels at your favorite bookseller or library and discover them for yourself. Start with ERNEST & REBECCA #1 "My Best Friend is a Germ" and continue on through graphic novels 2-5. In the fifth book, "The School of Nonsense," six-and-a-half year-old Rebecca joins her teacher, Mr. Rebaud, in a minor revolt against the school principal, who sensibly ordered the teacher and his students inside out of the rain, but he refused. The following page features Rebecca, Mr. Rebaud, and a few of her fellow students rejoicing in the rain. While this is indeed a very dumb thing to do, this page is beautiful example of great comic art by writer Guillaume Bianco and artist Antonello Dalena. I hope you like it. Consider it the cherry on top of the delicious desert that is DANCE CLASS!

For more great comic art, you won't want to miss DANCE CLASS #10 by Béka and Crip. So until next time, class dismissed!

Thanks,

Jim

"A little silhouetto of a man"

Guillaume Bianco
Antonello Dalena
Ernest & Rebecca
5
The School of Nonsense
PAPERCUTZ

STAY IN TOUCH!

EMAIL: salicrup@papercutz.com
WEB: www.papercutz.com
TWITTER: @papercutzgn
FACEBOOK: PAPERCUTZGRAPHICNOVELS
MAIL: Papercutz, 160 Broadway, Suite 700, East Wing, New York, NY 10038

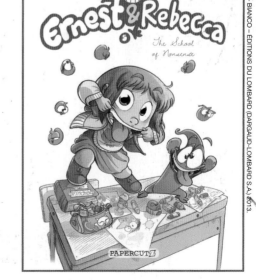

As described on the previous page, here's a beautiful scene from ERNEST & REBECCA #5…

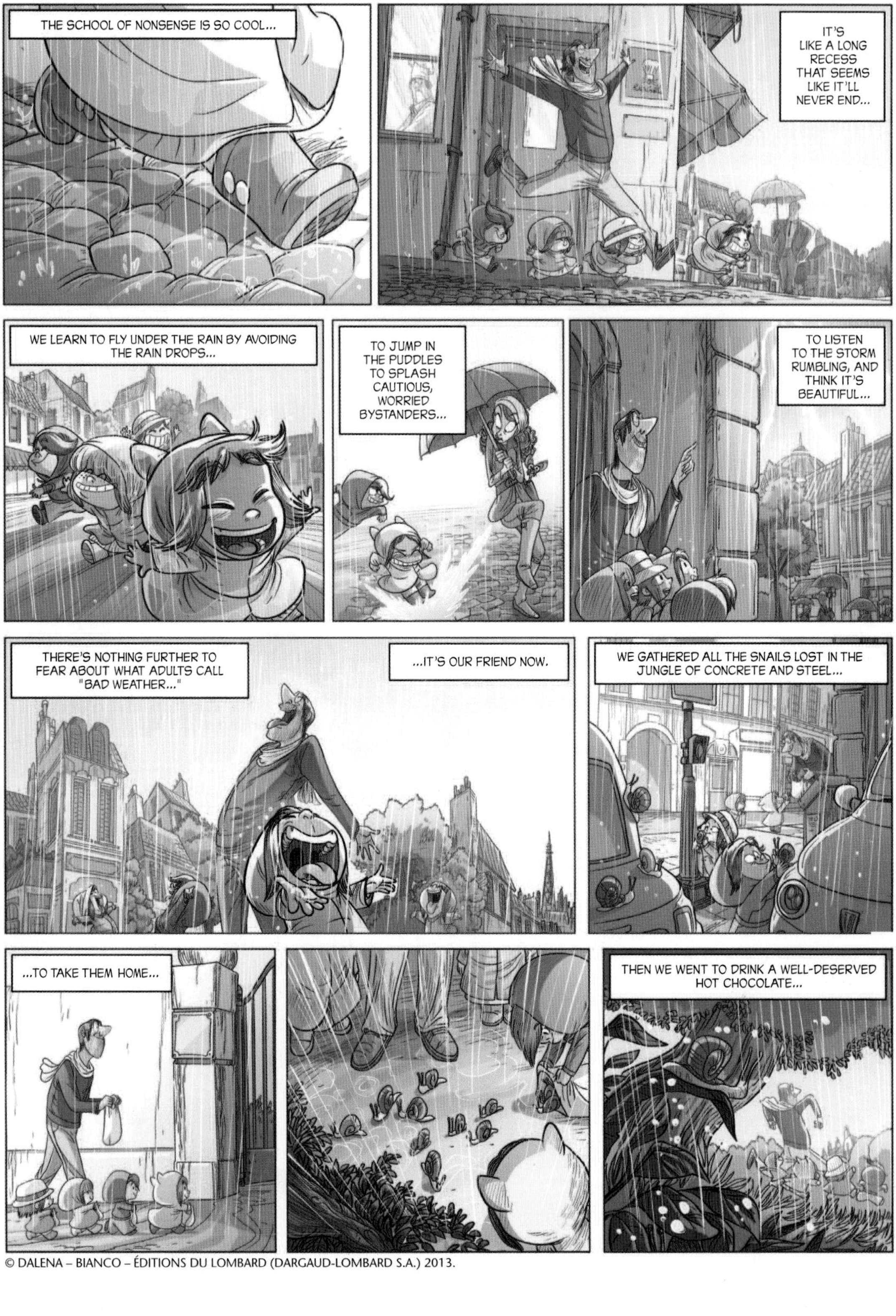
THE SCHOOL OF NONSENSE IS SO COOL...
IT'S LIKE A LONG RECESS THAT SEEMS LIKE IT'LL NEVER END...
WE LEARN TO FLY UNDER THE RAIN BY AVOIDING THE RAIN DROPS...
TO JUMP IN THE PUDDLES TO SPLASH CAUTIOUS, WORRIED BYSTANDERS...
TO LISTEN TO THE STORM RUMBLING, AND THINK IT'S BEAUTIFUL...
THERE'S NOTHING FURTHER TO FEAR ABOUT WHAT ADULTS CALL "BAD WEATHER..."
...IT'S OUR FRIEND NOW.
WE GATHERED ALL THE SNAILS LOST IN THE JUNGLE OF CONCRETE AND STEEL...
...TO TAKE THEM HOME...
THEN WE WENT TO DRINK A WELL-DESERVED HOT CHOCOLATE...